THE ENGAGEMENT PLAN

G.L. TOMAS

ISBN 13: 978-1-943773-54-1 (e-book)

ISBN 13: 978-1-943773-55-8 (paperback)

ASIN: B08QRSTSJ9

❀ Created with Vellum

SUMMARY

Evan Cattaneo was used to getting what he wanted.

The successful career. Check.

The Penthouse apartment overlooking the city. Check.

Let's not forget the drop-dead gorgeous girlfriend. Triple Check.

Only now, being in the relationship of his dreams, he discovers one slight problem that puts a dent in his plans for the future. His girlfriend Luz doesn't see herself getting hitched. Forcing Evan to confront their differences and understand their conflicting ideas to aid in his engagement plan.

A trip across the country, some much-needed therapy and their ability to work together as a couple fit into that neat little package. Only the closer he comes to uncovering the truth behind her reasons, he learns a devastating secret that will affect the state of their once happy union.

Note: This is The Engagement Plan, Book Two in the Love Unexpected Series. If you've found yourself trying this out of sequence, it is best if you backtrack to The Love Bet as the reading experience is improved by reading in sequence!

CHAPTER ONE

Evan

People always talk about first loves. Destiny and the fantasy of having a soulmate; that one person who was meant for you. I used to think it was all a hoax. Fairytales fabricated by idealists trying to sell you a concept of happiness to keep you striving for the impossible.

For me, when it came to relationships, practicality always won. My mother and father were celebrating thirty plus years being married, but I was wise enough to know that what they had lasted so long because they worked well together and complimented each other. Perhaps they weren't wildly in love like the dream others try to sell you on. That's what I used to think.

Then I met the woman who changed my entire outlook on love.

Luz De Los Santos. From the first moment I laid eyes on her, I was a victim to Cupid's bow. At eighteen, perseverance won me her heart and last year, after a fifteen-year separation, we'd rekindled our brief teenage love affair for a more serious, future defining relationship.

From the time she'd moved in with me, we had been inseparable; integrating ourselves into each other's world's, finishing each other's sentences, and being the couple people had put money on that we were going to make it. Most people waited their entire lives to feel the way I felt about Luz and, being the lucky bastard I was, I got a second chance to do it right this time. I had no doubt in my mind that this woman was going to be my wife. Which was why I'd taken the afternoon off to meet with a jeweler.

Three weeks from now, on our one-year anniversary, I was going to ask Luz to marry me.

Allison Wang had come to me with high recommendations; half of my firm had commissioned her for anniversary gifts and engagement rings, and it didn't hurt that she iced out some well-known celebrities and socialites, so her waiting list was months long. I didn't want to take any chances, so while I didn't have a set budget in mind, I didn't want to be cheap about it either. My engagement plan had to be perfect.

Allison stepped out from a backroom to greet me in the lobby, the youthfulness in her appearance catching me off guard. Over-sized round glasses swallowed up half of her small face, big hoop gold earrings hung from her ears like chandeliers, and I'm sure if Luz were here, that would have been the first thing she'd compliment her on. With her medium length dark hair styled in a high ponytail, she looked more like an undergrad than an expert on diamonds but, given her work, she was one of the best artisan jewelers in the city, so I had to let go of my biases.

"Hello. Mr. Cattaneo, is it?" She motioned me closer to her row of display cases and gestured for me to sit across from her. "Would you like any tea? Coffee? Maybe a shot of bourbon?" she added in her native London accent without skipping a beat.

"You can call me Evan, and that's a no to all three. For this I kind of want a clear head, but thank you though. No wonder you come highly endorsed." Serene music played in the background as the owner took a seat on a gliding chair and slid over to me.

"So, what are we in the mood for today?" Casting my gaze down to the locked display cases, blinding diamonds and other precious stones caught my attention, but I wasn't certain what I was after. I just knew that when I saw it, I'd know, and so far, what was available didn't *scream* Luz.

"I'll be honest and say I know almost nothing about jewelry, but I know the kind my girlfriend wears all the time. She's sort of trendy, I think. So, the classic engagement ring isn't going to excite her. Do you have anything more on the unusual side?" A coy smile formed on her face as she pointed to me and stood up to head back to her office. When she returned, a tray of a dozen designs rested on her forearm before laying it down for me to get a better look.

"You mentioned on the phone that you would be hard to please, and rightfully so, seeing as how you're proposing soon. Right here is a newer, more avant-garde collection I collaborated on with a fellow designer. They focus on less traditional stones and settings, but if your partner is ahead of trends, I could see one of these working. Have a look."

Surrounded in a rich, plush purple velvet, a true artist dedicated to their craft set the glittering stones in impressive framework but even after a close examination, I wasn't good at hiding my contempt for them. They were a little *too* different. When I mentioned unusual, it didn't mean I wanted an engagement ring that reminded me of a class ring or something novelty. Eye-catching but down-to-earth. Luz wasn't going to wear something that "looked" too expensive. I could hear her voice now on how a high-priced engagement ring could've gone toward something more practical. It had to *be* expensive without looking like it. I'm sure that made no sense.

"Why don't you tell me a little more about your beloved? It helps to know some of their favorite things, what their interests are, peculiarities? I'm better at recommending things when I can paint a clear image."

What was there to say about Luz? In my eyes she was flawless. Not perfect in the literal sense that reduced her to her looks or body. My favorite things about her came in the form of her quirks, her flaws, her stubbornness, and the shit she did that worked my last nerve. My mom used to always say if you love someone as much as they annoy you, you won't find a love truer. I used to mark it as bullshit but here I was, both equally frustrated and completely smitten by her. It didn't get any realer than that.

"She's smart. Hilarious. I mean, this woman can make me laugh in my worst moods. She always makes the best Netflix recommendations. She calls herself weird but I don't think she she's weird, she just has interests that aren't traditionally explored by people of her culture. Aww man, she's unapologetically herself. That's one of the things I love about her. I'm Italian so her brazenness is something I love in her." If a woman wasn't challenging me every five seconds, I'd question her feelings for me. People who lived for your growth called you out on your shit. Luz was definitely that.

"And she's beautiful." I blushed, recalling all the reasons I loved my woman. Proud to prove it, I pulled out my phone and brought up my favorite photo of her curled up on the couch with Mary, our cane corso. According to Luz, her hair was a frizzy mess and she hadn't put on her face yet, but the pleas she made for me to delete it went unheard. To me, she never looked sexier.

"It's so helpful to know her skin tone. Some metals are more flattering than others, depending on your undertones and where you fall on the Fitzpatrick scale. I personally think you can't go wrong with platinum. It always looks stunning on women with dark to deep complexions."

I shrugged cluelessly. To me, Luz looked good in everything, but women had a sixth sense about these sorts of things. If she was suggesting it, she had a better eye for which colors looked flattering on different skin tones than I did. Only none of these rings she showed me reminded me of Luz's taste and what she might like. Maybe it was my fault. Maybe I was being too damn picky. What if I was reading too much into it? This morning I had it set in my mind that this would be the easiest thing I ever did but so far, it's been the opposite. Who knew ring shopping would be this draining?

Allison adjusted her retro glasses, the blue liner traced along her hooded eyes making her eye color appear a deep shade of aged whiskey. In a past life I would've thought she had beautiful eyes, but my addiction to a drug called Luz only made me compare them to hers. No one held a torch to my fiancée to be.

"It looks like we have nothing currently stocked that will satisfy your selective expectations. Since you mentioned working with a higher budget, we could always go custom. That way you choose the setting, the framework, the stones, and all the intricate details. Whatever you envision in your head, I'm sure I can recreate as long as it's realistic." Giving the suggestion more thought, I wondered why I didn't think of that. I had the money to invest and to me she was worth it. That settled it!

"You know what? Let's do it! Let's build a ring from scratch."

CHAPTER TWO

Evan

At the start of my day, I was nothing but confident. Aside from being rewarded to some of the most *amazing* morning sex, my time at work had flown by with a stack full of successful closings that would mean more commissions to put toward our home saving fund. Today had just been one of those days where everything had seemed to be going right, that is, until it was time to get ready for our anniversary date.

Fear and anxiety had taken over, and it was hard not to show it when I'd lost sight of our dinner plans and was driving so fast I got pulled over, making us ten minutes late for our celebratory reservations. Luz had brushed it off at first, chalking it up to me having a stressful day at work, but when we were sitting across from each other at a five-star Michelin restaurant, it took a quick snap of her manicured fingers to remind me where I was and what we were celebrating.

"Earth to Evan. Gosh, papi. What's up with you tonight? Ever since we left the apartment you've been acting a little off." Holy shit, she looked so gorgeous tonight with her normally thick curly hair pulled back into a conservative low bun. As much as I loved to admire her thick display of curls, this style definitely reminded me of how aesthetically stunning she was without her hair fighting for competition for her beauty.

"I would have been content with a night in, but it was you who insisted we *had* to go out." Scooting my chair to her side, my nerves calmed closing the distance between us.

"That's because I love showing off my beautiful girlfriend. Especially when she looks as good as she does now," I said, planting a kiss on her bare shoulder, her skin goose bumping at the spot. She was wearing this sexy dark green halter dress that made her tits look incredible and the slit on her right leg screamed old school Hollywood glamour. Watching her get ready had been an absolute test of my willpower. Maybe fucking before we got here would have eased my stress a bit. Note to self, anytime you're making an important decision that can change your life, fuck first.

"Great! Then you don't mind if your beautiful *girlfriend* takes a piece of your steak." Not even waiting to get my blessing, her greedy knife and fork cut off a piece of my dinner only seconds after the waiter brought out our food. One of the things I loved about Luz was that she was so good at distracting me when something weighed heavy on my mind. The downside was that she did this every time we went out and it annoyed the shit out of me. It did give me something to nag her about, and when I was nagging, I wasn't worrying.

"Luz. Why don't you just order the steak like I always do? You always get the weirdest thing on the menu and complain the whole time that you didn't like it." Her face transformed into an irritated grimace, cutting off another piece of steak I hadn't even touched yet.

"Damn, so it's my fault that I want to try different things. I don't care where we go. Korean, Brazilian, Argentinian, you're like an old man. Your ass always gets the steak." My eyes widened at her clear attack on my ongoing staple.

"Yeah, because I always fuck it up." Why switch it up when I knew I'd regret not getting my go to?

"What I got isn't so bad," she said in between chews. "It's just in this case the steak is definitely better." How would I know? I never even got to try it.

"Here, try some." She cut off a generous helping and spoon fed me part of her cream sauce-based duck. Damn, it was good. Better than good. Why the hell was she eating off my plate?

"Thanks, baby," I said, grateful to her dusting off a dab of food left behind by her sample. She tugged at my beard, something she habitually did as I was debating on trimming it or letting it grow out. I was currently undecided.

"I swear, when you wear your beard like this, you look just like..." Before she could further work my patience, I cut her off with a fair warning.

"Don't say it."

"But why? It's such a compliment. You know I don't be having celebrity crushes like that. So, you know Massimo must have been putting in that work." Wrinkling my nose, I struggled to find the right words.

"Okay, so how would you feel if I said that you looked like my celebrity crush?" I asked as she casually shrugged. I didn't really have a celebrity crush. I was too busy and too enamored with my real-life crush, but Luz was one of those pop culture nuts who knew everyone's name in every piece of work they'd ever done. A common thing to sell her on a show was for her to know who was in it. Depending on the answer determined whether or not she would find that show worthy. I just liked a good plot.

"That's the difference between us, Luz. I don't have one. Besides, you don't really look like any actresses I can think of except maybe that girl on the show you liked. The one about the kids and the roller world plot." She blinked her eyes in confusion, her fingers spreading out like a fan in front of her chest.

"*Wowwwwww*. So you think I look like Monse from *On My Block?*"

"Well, not *now,* because she's playing a girl in high school, but she reminds me of the way you looked when we were kids." Her dark eyes reduced the slits.

"Okay, but she's like, three shades lighter than me. Definitely more light skinned than brown skinned." When Luz got to talking about the differences in skin shade, it was always a clear reminder that I was White and did *not* think about stuff like that. But it was an eye-opening topic of conversation, something I never failed to learn something new from whenever she brought it up.

"I didn't say she was your twin. I meant you favor her. Plus, she's really angsty like a certain someone was. That you *can't* deny," I challenged as she took a generous sip of her fruit infused water.

"Okay so I agree with that, but the only reason why there are no actresses who resemble me is because Netflix has a paper bag test problem. Your ass darker than a paper bag, you need not apply. Now my cousin Demeter, she gets compared to every light skinned black girl in Hollywood. *Shit*, I wish I had that problem, but I know she hates that shit."

"Not as much as I hate when you call me Massimo." Luz had made the ultimate mistake of calling me Massimo two seconds away from a nut after she practically *begged* me to watch *365 DNI* with her. It's one thing to call someone else's name when you're in the middle of fucking someone's brains out, but add insult to injury for it to be a fictional character. Ever since then I'd rejected the comparison. Maybe we had similar enough features to warrant it. Italian background, facial hair, lighter eyes, and tall, but nothing—and I mean *nothing*—kills the vibe more than your girlfriend lusting over a fictional character who, in a realistic setting, she would never go for.

"*Anyways,*" she declared as a warning that she was changing this subject. "There's this shelter in Queens that has a lot more breeds to choose from. They even list a lot of them on their website, and you can read their sweet little backstories. One of the girls at my job was telling me where she adopted her breed from and now I can't stop thinking about pitbulls. I hadn't realized how cute pits were." Sure they were cute but like cane corsos, they got into everything when they got bored. I couldn't imagine what their puppies would be like.

"Baby, I'm not so sure I want a litter of cane corso/pit bull mixes. If you think Mary is hyper, wait until she gets around a pit bull. Temperament is important." For the past few months, we'd discussed expanding our dog family, and after months of me saying no, I finally gave in. Luz had never had the privilege of owning animals before and as much as she and Miss Mary Mack had bonded, she longed for the chance where she could raise a puppy from birth.

"I know, I'm just excited when we do grown up things together." She pulled her phone out of her bag, her fingers typing rapidly on the screen to unlock it. She had already started making photo albums dedicated to all the breeds she liked that she saved from Pinterest. Clicking on the one titled pits, she scrolled through the album, certain to make me aware of all the ones she saved of them smiling.

"You can't tell me those don't look cute," she whined, and all I could do was roll my eyes.

"Yeah, Luz, they *look* cute. But watch when we've got two overactive dogs running around that's only going to get more hectic when they start having babies. Hell, we might have to even puppy proof the house." When our waitress stealthily crept up behind me, I jumped back in surprise at her clear but delicate speaking voice, causing Luz's expression face to scrunch in a fit of awkwardness.

"Hello again. How is everything? Would you like some more sparkling water?"

"You know what? Everything's great, but do you know what we could really go for? You wouldn't happy to carry Chateau Carrudes De Lafite Pauillac on hand, would you?" I asked, knowing it was Luz's favorite, and the first sign of her smile put my nerves at ease. Indulging at a few wine countries, Luz had picked up a liking to imported French wine, so whenever we did the fancy date night ritual, I never failed to buy her a bottle.

"I'll have to double check on that one, but I'm sure we do."

She attempted to rush off to fulfill my request but stepped back when I grabbed her attention. "Actually, if you do have it, do you mind bringing us a bottle? It's our anniversary and it's *kind of* her favorite."

"Oh my god, congratulations on your anniversary. Now I *have* to find it. Do you mind giving me a little time to look?" she asked, placing her little notebook and pen in the pockets of her apron when I gestured yes. As I turned back to Luz, excitement brought her rose painted pout into a smile, her palms pressed together in a prayer while her oversized hoop earrings swayed back and forth as she shook her head.

"Oh, my man is pulling out all the stops tonight. I hope they have it," she squealed. Fuck, there go my nerves again. Could the waitress get back any faster? What I needed was a drink. A tall glass of wine would loosen me right up, but I knew I didn't have all night. Eventually, I was going to have to man up and do what I came here to do. Literally the only thing standing in the way of me having a nervous breakdown was the soft felt texture of stroking the ring box I had stashed in my pocket. I wasn't going to wait for the waitress to come back with the wine. It was either now or never.

Adjusting in my seat, I kneeled to the floor on one knee, my hands seconds away from pulling out the ring box, and trying to get Luz's attention. Only the screams from a nearby table had forced everyone's gaze to our neighbors next door.

"Sweetheart. I've waited my entire life to meet someone who

makes me want to hang up my player ways. You're the only one that's been able to tame me," could be heard from the man in the burgundy tailored suit as he proposed to what appeared to be his long-term boyfriend. The ohhs and the awws, the collection of people taking out their phones to record their magical moment (Luz included), had been the tipping point of a catastrophic disaster. I couldn't propose *now*. Not after an epic commotion like that.

"Oh my god, Evan, do you see this? They are the cutest couple ever. I thought moments like this never happened in real life." Her brows furrowed in confusion when she finally looked back to center her attention on me. Pretending to tie my shoe laces, I stood back up and took a napkin from the table to wipe down my sweaty palms. "Hey, is everything okay?" I nodded hoping I didn't look as anxious as I felt.

"Yeah, yeah, everything's fine. I just dropped something," I lied, stuffing my face with a forkful of eggplant.

"Ah, baby, you missed it. It's okay because I got it on video." Turning her chair around, she once again congratulated the couple and spent almost ten minutes getting to know everything she could about them and where she can send the video if they wanted to share it with their friends and family. Don't get me wrong, I love that she was gregarious and celebrated her queer brethren any and every way she could, but she did *not* have to ask for an invite to their future gift registry.

I was already on glass two of her favorite wine before she turned back around and noticed. *Huhhh*...there went my engagement plan.

"Oh, nice, they have it. Why didn't you just scoot over and grab me?" she asked, oblivious to the fact that if I had been one minute earlier, it would have been *us* people were congratulating and recording on their cell phones. What was I saying? I still had the rest of the night. There was still time to plan something else special. Perhaps it wouldn't be the public proposal I wanted it to be, but with three hours left in our anniversary, by midnight's time, Luz was going to be my fiancée.

***

The drive back into the city had done wonders for my anxiety. No, I wasn't one hundred percent there yet, but I had a whole twenty minutes before we reached Chelsea, not to mention a soothing playlist filled with the Luz approved rock songs she made for me every time we planned a car ride out of the boroughs.

"Oh, I almost forgot. I got you a card." She snapped her fingers, digging through her oversized purse. From the corner of my eye, I couldn't make out the design but the two of us had agreed that with the new dog in our future, and vacation time coming up, we were limiting our spending until we decided where we'd go. The card was just as good as any gift and hopefully the custom engagement ring I got cancelled out the fact that we weren't giving each other gifts. Trying to keep my eyes on the road and look at the card, I read the greeting back to myself, grateful for the red light so I could give it a read through.

"To my sexy lover. I can list a million and one reasons I fell for you. Is it your charm? *Sure.* Your personality? *Absolutely.* Your glowing smile? *Close but not quite.* Okay?" I questioned glancing up at the light to make sure it hadn't turned green yet.

"The real reason is inside." Opening the card, I was met with a pop out mesh eggplant that almost made me choke. "It was the D, It was all for the D. Luz, where did you even find a card like this?" I laughed, shifting the car to second gear as she reached in before the card fell to the floor.

"I thought it was cute and funny. It wasn't like I could buy you anything, so I spent twenty-five bucks on a quirky card to make you laugh." Taking her left hand into my right, I kissed her fingers, wondering how I got so lucky to have such a sweet girlfriend. She was not afraid to be the geek I'd fallen in love with in high school and I loved her for it. Didn't I read somewhere that laughing burns five calories for every three minutes of painful laughter? If so, Luz was going to keep me fit for ages.

"Anyways, tonight was amazing, papi. Thanks so much for convincing me to go out. I got a chance to wear this up and coming designer's dress Gen let me borrow from the fashion department." She added a shimmy to emphasize her love for the dress. Even in a dim light, the rich deep emerald looked striking against her warm brown skin.

"Did you really think of tonight as amazing?" I asked curiously. By my measurement, everything that could have gone wrong did, but perhaps she had a different standpoint, considering it was just another date night in her eyes. "What part of the night stood out to you?" She unlocked her hand from mine to caress the fabric of my suited shoulder.

"Well, for starters, *you* in a sexy ass suit. I have a habit of normalizing your everyday work suits, but your date night suits? Oh, they just give me the chills." An arrogant grin formed at the corner of my lips when she expressed her unique version of complimenting. If only some woman knew how far a compliment went, even if you've been dating for years and stuck in a comfort zone. Luckily Luz didn't have that problem.

"For French food, it was amazing. You know I prefer Mom and Pop spots because they give you more food for less, but that creamy wine sauce over seasoned duck has me googling something similar so we don't have to go all the way back to Connecticut to eat it again. *Of course*, I can't find anything." Bringing her phone close to her face, her expression switched from excited to disappointment to learn the recipe she googled was made with chicken instead of duck. She slapped her palm on her knee and turned pointing a manicured nail in my direction.

"Oh, you know what else I loved? That couple sitting next to us getting engaged. When older queer couples' get engaged, I don't know, it's just super dope. I felt excited for them. I mean, not that I'm the biggest fan of the idea of marriage itself, but it's people's choice if they wanted to walk barefoot and headfirst into the hell mouth of misery."

"Hell mouth of misery? That's kind of harsh," I challenged but her never backing down to share her opinion, she dug herself in a deeper hole with her next explanation.

"How so? Most millennials aren't even getting married and Gen Z's are even more savage than we are. When people *do* get married, it's just so they can flex on their social medias, bragging about how perfect and happy they are only to divorce a year later. Trust me, I've collected the data. People treat marriage like it's returning a pair of shoes you don't like. In this day and age, marriage isn't for everyone." Her last statement crushing what was left of my confidence and nerve. I had no idea that she felt that way. Until today, the talk of marriage had never come up because I was waiting for the right time. Now, I wasn't sure there would ever be a right time.

"Evan, you know I'm pro-love, pro-relationships, pro-monogamy, and all those other things I thought I couldn't adhere to until we got back together, but marriage takes great couples' and makes them shitty people sometimes. Look at us. We have our squabbles occasionally, but ninety-five percent of the time we're healthy and happy. We don't need a piece of paper to define how serious we are about each other. It's just prehistoric and old fashioned." Without having to drag it out of her, I had the answer to the question I failed to ask. Luz wasn't going to say yes. And she wasn't going to marry me.

CHAPTER THREE

Evan

Tonight had been a reminder that no matter how well you plotted out your life plan, there was always something to remind you that fate had other plans for you. *First*, I lose the nerve to propose. *Then*, I find out my live-in girlfriend didn't see marriage in her long-term future. To make matters worse, Miss Mary Mack took her sweet time on the late night walk I took her on when we got back knowing I had an early day in the morning. *Okay*, so maybe Mary didn't know or care about the hectic day I was going to have at work tomorrow, but damn. Weren't there any woman in my life that didn't want to make it more difficult?

Luckily, when we got back from the walk, Mary didn't give me any hassle getting her turned in for the night, and given how quiet the apartment was, I assumed Luz was already fast asleep. Heading toward the bathroom, a quick shower was in order to rinse away the rest of the negativity and self-doubt lingering in my thoughts at the memory of Luz's words.

She didn't want to get married. How the hell did we spend the past year together and that had never come up? Moving in with me had brought a point of healthy dependency that I personally thought would take us longer to achieve. In the past year, she had gotten better at opening up and admitting how much she needed me, something that considering how independent she was, was hard for her to do. I had finally gotten her to let her guard down, embracing all the love and security I made available when I was all in with a relationship. But with all our milestones, fancy trips, and daily routines, it finally dawned on me how little we discussed things that felt inevitable for how our relationship was evolving. For men who were truly invested in a relationship, we didn't take years to make our dream girls our wives. All I needed was a few months and I knew she was my person.

But learning she only saw it as a piece of paper forced me to examine if the futures we saw together were two different futures. She definitely wanted kids. Believe it or not, being around my boys, that was the one thing we *did* talk about all the time. She made me promise her if we did, we'd moved to the suburbs because kids deserved to have backyards and tree houses and an overall safe place to call home. My naiveté assumed that came with the promise of matrimony. In the end, one of us was going to end up settling.

Securing a large towel around my waist, I opted for a hand cloth to dry my damp hair and tossed it in the hamper before hightailing it to bed.

Only when I opened the bedroom door, my mouth dropped to the fucking floor, and my eyes...my eyes didn't see anything but her.

"Wow," was all I could manage before taking her all in and letting pessimistic thoughts escape me. A naughty red mesh and fishnet lingerie set hugged her trim body with matching sheer thigh highs stockings making use of her svelte long legs. With long gloved hands, she held a red riding crop with a fitting heart at the end of it in one hand and what looked like a silk blindfold in the other. If she was wearing shoes, I couldn't tell you what kind because she looked so sexy, I was ready to maul her right then and there.

"Fuck, you look hot. Like a wicked, evil, *sexy* dominatrix." I leaned in to kiss her only to be met with her gloved finger pressed against my lips to keep me at bay.

"You like?"

"*I love!*" I said way too enthusiastically, remembering that Luz wasn't big on lingerie since she found them uncomfortable, but being grateful she compromised in that area because of how much I liked it. Every special occasion we've celebrated since being together, she's surprised me in something I loved her in. This set was doing its job *just* like the others because if we didn't get started soon, I was five seconds short of ripping it right off of her. "I'm a huge fan of these things." I pointed to the hearts over her nipples, biting my lip at how easily they came off with just a stroke of a finger. "And would you look at that, they come off. Just like this whole thing is coming off," I said snapping off a piece of her garter as her crop met my wrist in an unwelcomed slap.

"Oww!" I retracted my hand, it finally sinking in that we were next to eye level, so she was definitely wearing heels. Taking my chin into her silk covered hands, she caressed my face as a flirty smile formed at the corner of her mouth that made my cock rock hard. My woman owned her sexuality and owned me any and every time she let me know she wanted me as much as I wanted her. That was always the biggest fucking turn on.

"Relax, Evan. Don't be in such a rush to fly through our anniversary. You seemed so distracted at dinner. Let me treat you to some late-night dessert." Pulling me over to the bed, it became more evident how much thought and effort she put into this. Rose petals were practically everywhere and, not too far from where she sat me down, was a collection of her tools and acces- sories she liked to keep handy when she was taking the lead and willing to make the intimacy all the more memorable. If she was good at anything, it was opening up my mind to all the ways pleasure went neglected on a man and I wasn't going back for anyone. Not with all the things she helped change my mind about.

With a big dopey grin forming on my lips, I took a quick glance at her toys as she leaned in to sit on my lap and bless me with her dick hardening neck kisses.

"That black one over there? Is that what I think it is?" Her bite to my shoulder was telling me everything I needed to know.

"Mmmhmm...I figured we . . . " With a forceful tug to my hair, she pulled my head back and tapped a gloved finger to the tip of my nose. "Could spend a little time with a little massage. Give that neglected prostrate a little much needed attention," she cooed, leaning into kiss me as I wrapped my arms around her and gave her ass a big squeeze before she pushed me down and sauntered off the bed.

Before Luz, I'd never let anyone near my ass, but with what felt like expert debating skills, she had finally persuaded me to let her help me achieve my first prostrate orgasm. In her words, pleasure wasn't queer or straight. The prostrate was the male equivalent to the infamous G-spot on a woman, so there shouldn't have been shame attached to enjoying one.

The first time she worked her magic on me, I was so nervous, my dick could barely get hard. Once I felt safe enough to, I came so hard, my legs could barely hold me up the next day. Examples like that made me understand just how comfortable Luz had made me. She made more confident trying new things. While I didn't question how certain things related to my version of masculinity, it gave me great pride to have what every man wants in a woman. Not to mention, I was certain I was everything she wanted in a man.

"First, I'm going to do a little strip tease." She sashayed over to the stereo, lingering on a smooth jazz inspired Afro-beat song. With all the confidence in Manhattan, Luz swayed back over to me, and I helped her out of her sky-high heels. The second she turned her back to me, my hand instinctively smacked her ass, something that resulted in Luz making me pay for it with another smack to the back of my hand.

"I'm sorry, is this not interactive?" I teased. "Am I to keep my hands to myself?" Pulling her closer, I planted kisses on the part of her stomach that was free of lingerie. I was trying to forget about tonight, and nothing would make me more forgetful than being face first between a woman's thighs.

"No, but I'm trying to set the mood and here your horny ass goes and tries to mess up my flow." With her back to me, she lowered with a seductive whine, gyrating and grinding on my lap with only my damp towel between us.

She was the only one who was critical of her body. Thinking her ass wasn't big enough or that her thighs weren't thick enough. All I saw was perfection when I looked at her. There wasn't a moment I could resist my hands being all over her and pulling her into my lap, my towel opened up, revealing an insanely massive hard on, ripe for the taking.

"I don't know, baby. I'm not sure I'm getting the vision. Practically twerking in my face should be grounds for getting your ass smacked. Plus, I like the thing you've got going back here." Referring to the barely there V-string and fishnet garter. Why was it a sight to see? Because it left *nothing* to the imagination.

Breathing in her scent, the traces of Moroccan Argan Oil emanating from her hair was widely intoxicating. Not to mention her skin tasted like vanilla, cinnamon, and pheromones. I wasn't sure how long I could last like this.

A quick sweat session would solve that without question, but she was feeling bossy and the best thing to do was just sit back and enjoy the ride. Luz's lips on my skin was always a surefire way to drive me to the deep end. Between the tug of my nipples between her teeth and the way she seductively trailed a line of kisses down my navel, a part of me was losing my patience.

Teasing didn't begin to scratch the surface on how this woman took her time on all things sexual, but when she came back up to meet my lips in a ravenous kiss, the blindfold she secured over my eyes told me she was about to do some play below the belt.

The blindfold was more for me than her. There was always this wave of self-consciousness I had anytime we engaged in acts that ventured past the standard vanilla. Stripping me of my vision helped me relax and ease into the moment. "Mmm ...you're so clean, papi," she said, alternating between kisses to my neck and ear.

This girl knew all my detonators.

"Why don't we find a way to fix that?" Together, mouths never breaking form, we'd made our way to the middle of the bed, the rough cagey feel of the fishnet undergarment tickling my bare skin. Not looking forward to breaking free of our kisses, when we finally did separate, it was only to surprise me with her new toy. Luz's lips drifted all along my skin and torso, as I sensed her sitting up, reaching for her treasure trove of pleasure enhancers.

The sound of her a cap flipping open and squirting what sounded like a generous amount of lube seemed to drown out whatever song was queued next on her playlist. It was her words that assured me that it would be like every time before.

"So, some background on this one; it's gonna feel a little different from the other toy I've been using because it's meant to stay in place. Good news, though? We can have sex while you wear it." Sounded good to me.

"Ready?" she asked, taking my nod as her confirmation, as she took her time but totally went for it. I winced like I always do at the invading thickness that suddenly filled me.

"How's that feel?" There was concern in her voice.

"Ehh...about the same as it always does at first." With a flip of a controller, the toy inside me roared to life, causing my body to jerk at the unexpected sensation.

"Wow, I wasn't expecting that. Does it adjust? For the first few minutes, it feels way too strong." I didn't know how women set their vibrators to the highest setting without losing all feeling in their nether regions, but me personally, preferred something relaxed and subtle. Something that wouldn't distract me should we segue into fucking.

With a little tinkering on her end, she reduced the pulse speed to a manageable setting and didn't waste time gripping the base of my cock, urging it to action before devouring me whole.

Tearing off the blindfold, I had the pleasure of watching Luz make a naughty mess of my length, my fingers knotting in her hair, as I worked her head up and down my shaft. Egging me on, she shot a lascivious wink, clearly getting off on my reaction. With all her precision and expertise, I was afraid I was going to explode before I was pronounced dead on the scene.

The one thing I loved about prostrate orgasms was that I could have sex right afterward, but the power of them put me to sleep, so if I wanted to fuck, I had to stop her *now*.

It was tempting to let her just keep going because holy shit, the stimulation felt amazing. Not wanting to waste my nut without having a chance to be inside her, I asserted there were times where I'd definitely be selfish, but this wasn't one of them.

"Come here, baby. I want to eat your pussy," I summoned, pulling her on top of me, her insatiable mouth begging to be kissed. Her hunger for me melded with mine for her as our lips wrestled for dominance and replaced all will with only one basic need. The desire to please.

"Let's get you out of this." Pulling the straps of her bra to her elbows, I nuzzled her tits savagely, licking and sucking at the tips as her voice grew heavy with primal heat. "Fuck, come on, I want you to sit on my face." Cradling her face in my hands, I took control of the kiss and guided her up my torso to where she was positioned perfectly above my shoulders. Even now I could smell the woman under her perfume. There was no hiding the musk of her arousal as the eager, impatient side of me didn't even bother taking her panties off, choosing to whisk them to the side as I regarded her pretty pussy.

"Did you get waxed?" Referring to the smooth surface aside from one landing strip of hair down the middle of her mound. While it wasn't my favorite look on her, I admired the sight of her smooth and bare with well-deserved appreciation. With bare I could see everything, and bare, I was going to be eating this pussy all night.

"Mmmhmm..." At the sign of a kiss she winced and giggled, reminding me of how much more sensitive she was when there was nothing to hide.

"Well, you didn't have to but it *does* look nice. *Mmm*...I bet it tastes nice too." She spread her legs wider, lowering onto my mouth with selfish ease. Circling my tongue around her swollen clit, I reached my hands to cup her breasts, her tits the perfect handfuls as I rolled and pinched her dusky tipped nipples. Drowning in her taste, I found myself focused on the moment. Nothing was more important to me than making that pussy come for me. I knew all her little tells when she was holding back, when she was close, even when she was frustrated at the change of pace or suction. Luz was not someone who liked to be edged. She wanted *all* the orgasms, no matter how big or small, and the best part about driving her crazy was when she had no control over her own actions. When she was there, there was no denying her, especially with my arms wrapped tight around her legs. There was nowhere else to go.

"You look so *sexy* when you lick my pussy." She moaned, her eyes clamping shut from the way I licked up and down and finally taking her clitoris between my lips as her body jerked from the sensation.

"You like riding my face, baby?" Her words reduced to wordless moans as she grabbed both sides of my face and ground her wet pussy across my mouth with frantic lust and vicious need. Her thighs clenched tighter around my head, thrashing and panting being the only announcements she could muster while moaning that she was close to climax.

"Oh God, Evan, I'm about to come," she cried, and as her body trembled, she arched into me one last time before her sweet release erupted on my ready tongue.

"You good, baby?" I checked in letting her adjust herself on top of me, hips lowering and a shared breathy sigh at the feel of her muscles gripping my hard cock. "You're spoiling me. Here, let's sit up a little bit. I feel the plug better when you sink down."

Letting her place a few pillows behind my back, we relaxed into a treacherous rhythm that left my body confused of which sensations to give into. On one hand, prostrate orgasms had long lasting effects on me and I could still manage an erection if I succumb to one. On the other hand, the way Luz rode me, it felt like a waste not to blow my precious seed inside her. After all, she was on the pill and we stopped strapping up months ago, both in agreement it that felt better to feel each other.

With every whisper of how good it felt and every moan of my name, an overwhelming ripple of pleasure pooled to the brink of my sanity. The way she bounced on my cock providing that pressure every time she met my hips, by now it was obvious that it was going to be the first over the second, coaxing me to increase the speed as I gripped her hips and prepared myself for land off.

"Oh, Papi, you feel so good. There isn't anything that could top this anniversary." That's right, it was our anniversary. A night that hadn't gone as planned because of my botched marriage proposal and discovering that Luz had such a contrasting opinion about tying the knot. Before I registered my actions, I lifted her off of me in the midst of my undoing, sending her forehead crashing into the headboard, followed by her howling screams and cries.

"Oh my god, Luz. Are you all right?" I tended to her to make sure she wasn't having a concussion. Fuck, fuck, fuck. This night was becoming the worst night of my entire life.

"Baby, let me see. Can I get you an ice pack?" With pouted lips, she confessed how much she'd appreciate that but even after my insistence that we head to the emergency room, she declined, not wanting to spend the rest of our anniversary in a hospital.

Shooting up from the bed, I ran to the kitchen, filling the only ice bag we owned to the rim and rushed back to find Luz looking at her forehead with a compact mirror, clear concern on her face.

"Come here, baby. Let me put some ice on it." Caressing the bump on her head that formed in my absence, I apologized a million times before she lay down and cornered me with a conversation I'd rather not have given the night we had.

"You know, Evan, all night something's been off and I can't for the life of me explain what it is. Before dinner you seemed to be all over the place. And then when we finally to the restaurant, you were even more distracted than usual. At first, I thought it was all in my head, but when we're fooling around, I've never seen you this careless. Did something happen today that I don't know about? Please tell me it's not just in my head because I'm literally paying for it with a welt the size of a lime." Here we go. It was either stay silent and forever hold my peace or let her know what was really going on with me.

Whether it was tonight or two weeks from now, she was going to find out eventually. "No. *Argh*. I mean yes." I stood up pacing from the closet to the bed. "No, to it not being in your head. Yes, to something else happening. Or rather *not* happening. Something you said just got to me. It threw me off." She sat up pulling her bra back up and adjusted the ice pack on her head as it competed with her thick tresses of coils.

"Something I said?" she asked with genuine confusion. Given that my distractions had cost her, I owed it to her to be honest. After all, there was no room for secrets and lies when you lived together. Avoiding the conversation wasn't even an option.

"It was about the whole marriage thing. Did you mean what you said about not wanting to get married?" She attempted to furrow her brows but winced at the pain of her bruise.

"Is that what this is all about? You're upset because I said I don't want to get married?"

"You say it so casually like it's no big deal...Honestly, the real reason I was off tonight was because I had planned to propose. I kept hyping myself up and psyching myself out. But when the people sitting next to us beat me to it, a part of me felt like I had missed my moment. Then I was going to ask when we got home. Now I'm glad I didn't go through with it because based on our conversation on the ride home, you wouldn't have said yes, anyways. I feel like such an idiot."

"Evan, I had no idea." From the time I reached adulthood, I only had four life goals that were set in stone. Secure the successful job. Find and marry the amazing woman. Buy said woman her dream house. And lastly, start a beautiful family. Luz was supposed to be that woman, and now I was beginning to believe we didn't have the same life goals and that was far more devastating than hearing no.

"Baby, I'm Italian. The topic of marriage is like asking me if I prefer homemade sauce to store bought sauce. The answer is obvious," I explained.

"Evan, we don't have to get married to have a great life together."

"You see, that's the second time you've said that. That you don't want to get married and the second time I disagree," I argued. There weren't many things after a year together that could make me angry but hearing marriage wasn't in our future was definitely one of them.

"Gosh, are we seriously arguing about this on our first anniversary—?" Before she could finish, I interrupted, as her face distorted in disappointment.

"Yes, we are arguing about this because it's clear we have opposing opinions about our future together." By now I was fuming, my anger rising, knowing I was possibly wasting my time investing in someone who didn't want the same things. Maybe my biological clock wasn't ticking, but for some naive reason I thought my life would be so different by now.

"Evan, will you please calm down?" I took a deep breath, reading the hurt in Luz's expression, and understanding that perhaps things were getting a little loud on my end.

"Baby. I don't mean to yell at you. I just I didn't know you had such a strong opinion on something that felt inevitable for us."

"You make it sound like I don't want to be with you. I've given up so much just for this." She gestured between the two of us.

"Yeah, but that's not enough for me," I shamefully admitted and watched her face sink as she took a deep breath to what I assumed was holding back her tears. I promised myself I would never make her cry again, and now I didn't even recognize myself. I definitely needed time to breathe. *Alone.*

"If you had given me the chance to explain myself, I would have been happy to fill you in, but now what difference will it make? You've already told me how you feel," Luz said, defeated. Slipping on some clothes and grabbing an extra blanket from the closet, it was clear neither one of us was open to discuss this, and I just wanted to get some sleep before I turned into a walking zombie. Wiping a stray tear from her eye, her gaze followed me as I approached the door of our bedroom. "Where are you going?"

"Listen, babe, I really have to get some sleep, and things are just real hostile right now. I'm going to just crash on the couch and please..." I knew if I didn't tell her to stay put, she would just follow me, and for now I wanted to leave the disagreement where it was.

"Just give me some space, okay? I'm sure this is hard for the both of us, but I just I thought by the end of the night I would be able to call you my fiancée." Without another word, I made my way out of our bedroom and got comfortable on the couch. For the first time since she moved in, we were going to bed mad at each other.

CHAPTER FOUR

Luz

I wasn't surprised to see Evan had left for the day by the time I'd gotten up. I tried my hardest to sleep it off, but I still hoped we could discuss things over breakfast, and at least mend the animosity between us before we had more time to discuss it. When my phone went off, alerting me with a few messages, I rushed to it, my shoulders slumping in disappointment that it was only my mom telling me to check up on my cousin since she saw on the news that all this crap was happening in California. Nada from Evan.

Maybe it was because we were still in the honeymoon phase, but my man was known to send me some racy texts that left me desperate for him all day. And this morning, I didn't even get a goodbye kiss. All because I was honest about what I really felt about marriage. I can't believe he had planned to propose. I mean, I know our relationship was great, but I didn't know marriage was his end game. We never talked about getting married because in my eyes, we are on the same page. We were happy. We were healthy, and we were whole. We didn't need to get hitched to prove we had a future together.

I'd already conquered my fear of being in a serious relationship, but after the hell a past ex put me through, I had no interest in going down that road again. I liked where we were before he went and decided he was going to propose to me. What was I supposed to do with that information?

Before I give it anymore thought, Miss Mary Mack came running into the kitchen looking for her morning meal. I hadn't even had my coffee yet, but it looked like she was the only one in this house who could stand being in the same room with me. Sisters over misters. *Although* she did have the tendency to switch sides whenever it was convenient. We're going to have to work on that once we got her a partner to mate with. She was going to find out real quick that one tiny mishap could land you in the dog house. Hmmm...maybe she might like that?

***

If there was anyone in this office, I was the coolest with, that award went to my work wife Genevieve. Like me, she was by passionate about her own department, and worked hard to make it an inclusive nontoxic environment to those below her. Despite being seven years younger, we both found common ground over our love for the latest Black Pink song along with everything and anything related to food. Whenever she brought in her mother's homemade Pho or Cahn Cua, she knew better to bring more than one serving for me. Today she'd brought in a hefty tin from a place that was unquestionably Caribbean, but as she pulled up to our usual table in the cafeteria, I had almost zero curiosity to ask what she was having. I was too busy being distracted by the *one* text Evan replied to me after I'd sent him a whole thread about how much I cared about him. My anxiety was dialed to a fucking one hundred right now.

"Luz, oh my god. You have to try this macaroni and cheese I got from this new vegan Jamaican spot that just opened up around the corner. I don't know what they do to make it taste so velvety, but this is my second time ordering from there, and now I can totally understand how some people can give up meat." She flipped her lustrous jet-black hair off her shoulder, her diamond drop earrings in the shape of little disco balls swinging with the motion. Up close, the precision of her navy-blue wing tipped lined monolids paired with a glimmering brown smoky eye made me wish I experimented more with different shadows, but she was *literally* the fashion director. She could wear a paper bag from Trader Joe's and make it look couture.

"Not that I'm saying I could give up meat, but I can see how others could. You want to try some?" She scooped up a mouthful of greens and held it up toward my mouth. It wasn't like me to turn down food, but it also wasn't like me to be conflicted with a thousand negative thoughts at once. On a side note, her fresh new set looked fantastic. I have to get stiletto nails next time I get my nails done.

"No, it's okay. Gen, why don't you enjoy your food? I had one of those refrigerated lunch bars so I'm not in the mood for anything heavy." After savoring her hearty pasta, she put down her fork and rested her chin on her fingers, gazing at me through suspicious eyes. My relationship with Gen wasn't as close as relationship with my best friend Candice, but we'd spent enough time together to be out of work pals. We had some things in common and she was definitely more my version of fun considering my bestie was more reserved. When I was single and on the dating scene, she was always quick to invite me to the latest lady bar when they were having some cheesy costume party she knew I wouldn't pass up on.

"Okay, something is up. First, you don't even *look* at my tray of food. Then you turn it down when I offer up a hefty sample. You never turn down food, so why don't you tell your wife what's wrong." Damn, was I that predictable?

"Girl, you know I hate to unload on you, especially when

you're having a good day." Taking a quick glance at her aluminum container, the curried chickpeas and brown stew chunks were calling me. Maybe I would feel better if I got some real food in me. I mean, I couldn't feel any worse.

"You know what? Let me get some of those chickpeas." Handing me a utensil set wrapped in plastic, I tore it open and helped myself to her Caribbean feast.

"See, I knew you couldn't resist this curry. That's right, eat up and tell me the deal." As much as there was going on right now, from researching animal shelters to get Mary a man, I cut straight to the chase with my Evan dilemma, deep sigh included.

"It's about Evan." Resting her round cheeks in balled up fists, she took a sip of her smoothie.

"You mean that dreamboat *365 DNI* look alike you get to sleep next to every night? Ugh, don't tell me he's cheating or I'm gonna have to take a bat to his car and sort him out the Lower East Side way," she joked, as I informed her that that would *definitely* not be happening, given the history I had with tampering with Evan's car. With a mischievous smirk, she took another sip of her fruity drink. "Okay, *that's* a discussion for another day, but for now, what's your latest problem?"

"So it's definitely not cheating. Actually, it's the opposite. Yesterday when we were celebrating our anniversary, later that night, he told me he had planned on proposing. Only thing is he didn't because apparently, a couple sitting next to us had beat him to it. I guess he felt like it cheapened the moment. But then it gets worse. On the way home, we'd had this discussion about how I didn't see myself getting married but I didn't know he was going to propose so I was going *in. Then* he waits until we're moments away from seeing fucking Jupiter to give me this thing because I said something to trigger his botched plans." I pointed to the knot on my forehead that surprisingly looked a lot better from last night.

"We had this huge argument. He slept on the couch, which if

you knew him, he'd rather wake up to my snoring than sleep on the couch. And then this morning, he just leaves without saying goodbye. Now I just feel like we're in this weird place." Genevieve's eyes watered like she was moments away from crying, the word awwww passing her lips in an annoyingly longer time than I wanted to admit. When she saw I wasn't laughing, her sarcasm took over and changed her tune.

"I mean damn. *Nooooo*. Getting proposed to is bad. It is bad, *isn't it?*"

"No! I mean, yes. *Ugh!* I don't fucking know. All I know is that his feelings are hurt and he shuts down every time our issues aren't easily solvable. I don't know how to fix it." I groaned, stuffing another hefty serving in my mouth and letting my taste buds enjoy all the amazing seasonings that made this meal forget you weren't eating meat. Gen shrugged.

"I mean, you guys live together. Doesn't that make you feel married already?" That was beside the point and not the argument I was trying to make. Why do your friends always side with the person they know the least about? She was supposed to be sympathizing for me, not joining Evan's fan club.

"The way I see it, Evan is probably the most considerate guy I've met in real life from all the stuff you say about him. It's one of the main reasons I'm only dating women right now. All these guys from the boroughs are thoughtless and broke. The last girl I went out with, we were both practically fighting to pay for the tab. But the last date I went on with a guy, he pretty much itemized the receipt like he was filing his fucking his taxes. And get this, he still had the balls to ask if I wanted to head back to his place. I'm like, are you fucking kidding me?" That shit was hard to hear because Gen was a knockout. She pretty much had her pick in whoever she wanted, but she was picky since a lot of men fetishized her for being Southeast Asian. She got called every racist thing you could think of, most people not taking in consideration that she was Vietnamese and not East Asian like they assumed. We all had our own dating struggles, which made me appreciate in this moment that the one White person I've ever been in a serious relationship with never fetishized me. Why did he have to ruin everything by telling me he planned to propose?

"Damn, it's like I forgot what it's like to be out there. Sorry, Gen." I cringed.

"Yeah, so just know dating a Wall Street guy who sends you flowers every week on random days, coaches youth basketball, and looks like a Mediterranean prototype of the ultimate book boyfriend asking you to marry him doesn't sound like the worst thing in the world that can happen."

"So, at twenty-six you're telling me you actually *want* to be married?" With widened eyes, she lifted her hands appearing as though she was inches away from wanting to wrap them around my neck.

"Yes, if it means it's taking me off the market in a sea of bums. Listen, you're always going to be my work wife but I'd like a home wife. Or, if I can meet a guy like Vinh Nguyen, a home *husband*." With a high level of excitement, she banged her hands on the table making me to jump back in my chair.

"That's it!"

"Umm...what's it?" She rolled her eyes in the spacey kind of way she did when she was explaining something that should have been obvious.

"Not sure why I didn't think of this before, but you say you and Evan are in a bad place, right? Well, ever since my breakup with Jake JerkFace, I've been contemplating booking one of those intimacy retreats that are getting so popular."

In this huge confession, Gen had admitted to being in a weird spot when it came to putting herself first and figuring out how to get back to the person she was before a bad breakup last year. According to her, she had taken the plunge on attending motivational conferences, but that was getting her nowhere. She even caved and started taking femininity courses. The way she told it, it seemed to have helped her with self-esteem but she was still in limbo about whether she loved her current self enough to prioritize herself. From the outside looking in, I hadn't realized she was such a people pleaser where it affected her ability to say no. Bitch told me no all the time.

"Honestly, I wish I would have caved in and did the intimacy retreat venture first. Here, let me show you what I'm talking about." On her tablet she pulled up a YuVube channel of what looked to be a relationship advice coach. Obviously, the Hollywood kind because he was a ten in attractiveness, and I could practically see stars forming in Gen's eyes when she clicked on the link that led to his website's bio.

"So this guy hosts all these different kinds of retreats. One for singles, one for couples', even ones for families with children. I've been watching him *forever,* and between his dreamy eyes, sculpted torso, and shared cultural background, this man could make me join a cult if it sounded convincing enough." Clicking on his Instagram page, it wasn't hard to see what she saw in him. The guy was top tier fine. The kind of fine Buzzfeed wrote posts about when some newbie to non-Eurocentric men wanted to make a top ten list on Asian guys you're sleeping on. To me he was just attractive, race and ethnicity aside.

"Ummm...I'm not sure about this, Gen. Your pupils are all dilated. Your tongue is all out. If I'm being real, you look thirsty! And damn, twenty-five hundred bucks? That's a lot of damn money for a couples' retreat," I argued.

"Not for *your* boyfriend, it's not. And besides these retreats aren't located in some rented apartment building in a crappy area. He sets them in these beautiful locations where you have nothing but gorgeous scenery around you. It's hard to not want to fix your problems when you're surrounded by nature's wonders. Besides, Dr. Nguyen isn't some scammer. He's graduated from some amazing schools with multiple degrees, including a doctorate from Princeton in psychology. It's not like he can help being appealing to the eyes. He used to be a sex and relationship counselor, but now his brand is about sex positivity in families, how to build healthy platonic and romantic relationships. And look, he's even an expert on navigating kinky lifestyles. All you have to do is read one of his books or watch an hour of his view videos. He's the real deal."

Clicking on the tab where he typically hosted events like these, they were pretty inspiring and picturesque. I'm surprised Gen cared about that sort of thing, being born and raised in the city, and she rarely traveled beyond the boroughs. Between the retreat and the airfare, it would cost us about thirty-five hundred. But knowing Evan, spending money wasn't as serious to him as it was to me. When we booked a trip to Australia a few months prior, he barely looked at the prices, securing our first-class airfare and booked the nicest five-star hotel. The money wasn't the smoking gun.

It was the couples' therapy I knew he wouldn't be a fan of.

Evan had no issue seeing the importance of individual therapy, but *couples' counseling*? Let's just say in the time we were back together, he made it clear that Italian Americans hated people being in their relationships. To him, therapy counted as people being in his business. As hopeful as I was, there was still a chance he'd say no, which was why *I* had to get him to say yes.

CHAPTER FIVE

Luz

An immediate sense of relief washed over me the moment Candice and her half-sister Juliet came into view. As I inched closer to the bar, it wasn't hard to tell they shared at least *one* parent, despite having more differences in their appearance than similarities.

Juliet was the sister that their father had due to stepping out of his marriage, so Candice and Juliet were born within months of one another. It strained any relationship they would have had as kids and teens, but Candice was always trying to be the bridge between her two sisters. As an adult, Candice was the bigger person and reached out and has since become a support system for her niece's absentee father.

She built a relationship with Juliet, but that hadn't been the hard part. No, the real hard part was getting Candice, Juliet, *and* their eldest sister Marcia to hang out. *Together*. Hell, even I had only met Marcia once or twice.

As an only child, I didn't know what that was like, but I'd be lying if I didn't admit I had my own share of family drama. Since Candice was the bestie, I wanted nothing more than to make her sister feel welcome so I let her know that if Juliet ever had a free night she was more than welcome to join our girls' nights.

I'm actually surprised she never introduced me to her until a few months ago, she was real good people. Juliet wasn't as fortunate as us, so Candice always took Juliet's daughter over the weekend so she could get in some overtime, or at the very least, have a social life. Since I didn't have any siblings, there was definitely a hint of envy that Candice got a brand new one later in life. I shouldn't complain, though. At least I was getting a new friend out of it.

"Thanks for meeting with me, you guys," I said, pulling out a seat in between them so I was in the perfect range to hug both of them. "I know this isn't our usual spot but I had a million and one things to do and this was closer and—"

"Stop apologizing!" Juliet interrupted wearing a warm smile. "All I heard was happy hour was between two and four and I didn't need a lot of convincing on that one. That one, on the other hand." She accusingly pointed her thumb out at Candice.

"Girl, once the liquor set in, I wasn't tripping. You got a business, so you better mind it," Candice casually defended, sipping the bottom of what I hoped was her first mojito. These bitches knew they could have waited.

I only *slightly* forgave her because she had ordered for me once I texted I hadn't been far. For as bomb as the drinks were, it made up for it. Before I had arrived, they discovered the bar made a mean guava and passionfruit mojito, encompassing three of my favorite things. Guava, passionfruit, and rum. I didn't plan on going all out, but figured one serving of liquid courage would loosen me up more around my girls.

"I'm only doing one this afternoon, ladies, so enjoy me while you can," I stated firmly.

"One?" Juliet interrupted, surprised that *I* was the one who required a tamer time. If Candice was at a zero and I was at one hundred, Juliet would definitely fall somewhere in between, which was good balance. Only thing was, it rose suspicion when the turnt up friend suddenly wanted to turn the volume down.

"Yeah, I want to get a head start on dinner before Evan gets home. Especially since it takes forever to make his mother's sauce recipes. I swear they're no less than one hundred ingredients."

"Look at you, being all domestic," Candice teased. "You sure you're not trying to get married, because you sure are doing wife shit."

"It is not *wife* shit," I defended. "It's called being a team, which right now doesn't always feel like we're on the same one, but we're adults and we take turns cooking and tonight just happens to be my day."

"Well, if you want to get started, why don't we go back to your place and we could just hang out there. That way, we're not keeping you out. Plus side is you can just kick us out when the time comes." Juliet trying her best to sound like her suggestion wasn't personally motivated.

"*And* so she could hit up that well stocked bar at your place," Candice accused. "Yeah, bitch, you ain't slick."

"Hey, I'm just saying. Pay for more drinks, drink for free. Let me know what sounds better to y'all," Juliet defended, making a good argument. They were right. Evan did keep a lot of choices on hand at home for small gatherings, birthdays, and special occasions, so it came in handy for a little get together after work.

"You guys sure you wouldn't mind?" Grateful that they were okay with splitting a Lyft so that I would be home a lot earlier than planned. Luckily for us, home was only twenty minutes away if you counted the five-minute power walk we trekked to avoid traffic.

The moment we got home, Miss Mary Mack greeted me with the enthusiasm any cane corso would have when they've been left to their own devices most of the day. Considering the possibility that Evan needed some fresh air after work, I would leave him to do her evening walk just in case he hadn't cooled off.

"Damn, I keep forgetting how big your dog is. You sure she doesn't bite?" Juliet tensed, making sure she was close enough to a door just in case Miss Mary Mack approached her.

"Trust me, for as tough as she looks, she's more bark than bite. Especially now that we're on the lookout for a baby daddy for her," I joked.

Juliet curled her lips up. "I have one of those, and it ain't that great? She sure she wants one?" Juliet countered.

"We're in the process of expanding our dog family, so we're looking for someone she would be compatible with. We just want to start while she's young and healthy enough." Hell, while *we* were young and healthy enough.

"Juliet, you don't have to worry. She's a lazy attack dog," I confessed, slipping her some doggie treats before she pitter-pattered her way to her dog bed. "I'm convinced if we were ever getting robbed, she'd be the kind of dog to strike a deal just so she could get a cut," I joked.

"She's just big." Juliet said, trying to mask her discomfort. "I know owners get offended when you're scared of their dogs."

"No, I get it. She's actually the kind of dog who will avoid you if she senses you're afraid. She would much rather be adored by you than feared," I replied as I checked on Miss Mary Mack before she nodded off.

"Girl, you forgot your bonnet." I helped slip it back onto her head to be met with her fierce stare of annoyance. "Dulces sueños," I wished Mary, prompting Candice to laugh from her spot on the couch.

"That dog don't understand no damn Spanish," she chided.

"Okay, maybe she doesn't but she's learning," I whined. "Aren't you, girl?" A light scratch to her belly put her back to sleep in no time.

Careful not the low ball our alcoholic options but not pick any of the special occasion stuff, the three of us agreed on a wine that was fancy but modest. Not wanting to drink too much, I settled for a mini glass as I went in the kitchen to set up for Evan's favorite pasta sauce. For Evan, it was always less about the pasta and more about the sauce, so I was hoping his taste buds would be too satisfied for him to care whether we'd had a disagreement over the last day or two. That, or I was prepared to give mind-blowing head.

Following my well documented instructions, within a half hours' time, I lowered the temperature so it wouldn't stick to the sides of the pan. Filing a pan with water, I waited for it to come to a boil before throwing in some salt to flavor the pasta.

Girls Day was proving to be a nice distraction from the temporary problems plaguing my relationship. After a glass of wine or two, Candice and Juliet were playing music and debating on whose tempos were better, Cubans or Haitians.

Because she was technically Candice's *half*-sister, I had to keep reminding myself that Juliet was raised by her Haitian mom, and not the Cuban father who abandoned her. Both Juliet and Candice had button noses, but Juliet *definitely* favored her mother, because Juliet had fuller lips and much lighter skin. There was a lot of story regarding their pasts that neither of them were willing to share just yet, but hearing them defend which genres hit better, Kompa or Salsa made me glad I wasn't familiar with either. I wasn't trying to catch that smoke.

That wine must've been hitting too, because before I knew it, Juliet was lit enough to wake Miss Mary Mack up and attempt to teach her island-y moves associated with Kompa. Miss Mary Mack couldn't even learn Bachata, I doubted she had the discipline to learn Kompa.

It was just the entertainment I needed, to be honest. The mood was hype but not too hectic where we were getting calls from the neighbors. So when Evan walked through the front door, I was hoping that vibe would remain.

"Hey, Candice," Evan greeted her with a hug and kiss. "I'm guessing you're Juju."

"Juliet," she corrected before she held her hand for him to shake.

"Sorry about that. When Luz mentions you, she never called you by your full name. I've heard so much about you that I feel like I know you. I would hug you but I don't want to make things awkward or..."

"It's not awkward, I mean, outside the fact that I'm lit," Juliet joked. "This is your home, but I'm glad I'm finally getting to meet you." She smiled warmly.

Evan walked past the kitchen, but not before murmuring a low, "Thanks for getting dinner started," before announcing he was about to change out of his work clothes and disappeared into the hallway.

Candice and Juliet stood from their spots on the couch wearing those "Aight Imma head out" looks. "Maybe we should go. We don't want to get in the way," Candice said, being the first one to speak.

"You don't have to. I'm sure Evan wouldn't mind if you stayed for dinner."

"Maybe another time, you know? When things don't feel so tense." She'd sensed the mood change. "Thanks for the drinks, though," Juliet finished in more of a whisper, as they both came in to hug and kiss me on the cheek and quietly excuse themselves out the apartment.

Upon Evan's return, he managed to slip into appropriate loungewear that looked comfortable but wasn't too I'm-mad-at-my-girlfriend-so-let-me-throw-out-thirst-traps.

"Hey, where did the girls go? Did they know they were welcome to stay?" His tone had suggested that I had told them to leave.

"They did, they just had other plans and didn't want to be in our way."

"Oh," he said, confused. Instead of offering to help like he usually did, Evan galloped straight to the couch and turned on the

TV. It didn't even seem important, either. Weather and local news at best.

That wasn't like him at *all*. He was either still walking around with a bruised ego or he was intentionally being petty, both situations fueling me with equal annoyance. Evan was a great partner aside from the few things he suggested *I* do, that he never took his own advice on.

When I was upset, he'd push me to communicate, but when he was the one with issues, he'd just avoid me until he cooled off. If I didn't get him talking to air that mood out, I was going to be dealing with it all night. Making him come to me was the easiest part, but I didn't want to make it look obvious. While I didn't go this route often, with how predictable Evan was, there wasn't a doubt he'd come running.

Taking out the dry pasta I had planned to use for dinner, I brought it over the sink and started breaking it in half. There were only a few cardinal rules I had to follow now that we were living together, but there wasn't one that irritated him more that.

As a lifetime pasta breaker, I had never understood what the big deal was when it came to making sure the pasta all fit. In our blended Italian/Dominican-American home, Evan made it clear there was never a need to if you used the right pot. Since that pot was conveniently (and hypothetically) being borrowed by a neighbor, I had no choice but to use a smaller one.

With his supersonic hearing, Evan catapulted to the kitchen with a quickness that prevented me from even approaching my second batch.

"Luz, what are you doing?" he asked in frustration.

"I'm making the pasta fit better," I answered nonchalantly. If he was going to act silly, this game was for two players.

"Luz, come on. We talked about this. There isn't a need to break it when you're using the pasta pot."

"One of the neighbors asked to borrow it the other day, I figured you knew that," I said, acting none the wiser.

"No lie, Luz, that sounds like total bullshit—"

"Well, how else was I supposed to get your attention," I calmly interrupted. "From the moment you walked through the door, you ignored me. Getting on your nerves seems to be the only way for me to get you to say something that isn't 'thanks for getting dinner started'."

"Is this because I didn't offer to help you in the kitchen?" Pointing to himself like he was confused that I was frustrated.

"No. It's because you won't talk to me after…"

"After what? After I asked whether we were on the same page when it came to the future of our relationship?" He boldly met my energy.

"Hold up, just because I don't have the same opinions on marriage as you do, all of a sudden our relationship is in jeopardy?"

"Yes!" he yelled, despite later apologizing for doing so. He waited until he had calmed down before sharing his lingering thoughts about the other day.

"Luz, before yesterday, I thought I knew everything about you and what you wanted from me. What you wanted from us. Now I have doubts about everything. Is that what you wanted to hear?" His voice coming to a calm, rubbing the tension from his forehead.

Now he was scaring me. What about our relationship didn't sound final to him? We had moved in together, which was a bigger risk for me since I had given up my place and all my attachments to it. We decided to expand our dog family, not to mention having successfully integrated one another into each other's human families.

Everything we'd decided on and did together brought growth in our relationship. How could he say he had doubts about every-thing over *one* disagreement? "You have doubts about us?" I ques-tioned, my tone full of insecurity.

"Now I do," he shamefully admitted. "Maybe I'm dealing with

it in a way that you don't want me to, but I just need time. Maybe even space. I don't know."

"Space? What does that even mean?" I asked, caught off guard that he interrupted me again.

"I don't know. You want me to have the answer that will make you feel better, but we don't deal with things the same. I just need time to think...away from here."

"That just sounds so drastic."

"Luz, it doesn't to me. I respect how you deal with things. I'm asking for you to respect how I deal with things in my own way," he commanded before walking out of the kitchen. There wasn't more I could say. Asking for space was a new one for us. This problem was bigger than I thought. No amount of pussy or home cooked pasta was going to make him ease up how he felt on the subject. Maybe we did need that intimacy retreat after all.

CHAPTER SIX

Evan

Between Mary keeping Luz busy in the backseat and the psychedelic sounds of the Woodstock satellite rock station, it was the first time in days I got a few minutes to myself without Luz trying to smother me with her unsolicited advice columnist style sit downs.

She always complained about me bringing work back home but here she was going into Modern-Magazine-Mode trying to talk to me like one of her readers. Yesterday, I got lucky by coming home later than planned, so she hadn't had time to wear me down, like earlier in the week. However, today we had both taken off and while we had a busy day ahead of us, I was preparing for her to try attempt another sit down, since she hadn't gotten more out of me than "I don't want to talk about it."

I know our feelings about the subject weren't going to be resolved overnight, but this was one of those problems I wasn't even sure I had the language for. Frankly, I never thought I'd be in this situation.

Growing up, my dad and I had always joked about the down-sides of marriage, how most of the men in my huge Italian family did. When they weren't complaining about nagging wives, it was about troublesome kids, or obnoxious mother-in-laws.

Yeah, I always knew it was a crock of shit because for the most part, they were overall happy and couldn't see their lives without their families. Now that I was mature enough to articulate it, that was what I wanted. A family.

I had heard a dozen or so stories in my lifetime from my grandfathers, uncles, or cousins, about how they married the loves of their lives. They never made sense to me until I met the person I wanted that with, and it was hard knowing she might not become that next story. I didn't even know how to process that information.

"Hey, are we getting close?" Luz yelled over the music from the backseat. With Mary refusing to leave her lap until the car stopped, I knew she was just dying to walk around again. When the GPS signaled that the animal shelter was only a quarter mile ahead, I was thrilled to inform her that it'd be on our next left.

"You excited, girl? In a few minutes you will be mere feet away from finding your baby daddy," Luz said, Mary's face cupped in her hands. Mary would never get used to a time where she had to live without Luz's affection, and she certainly showed it with every tongue lashing to Luz's cheeks, drowning her in playful, wet kisses.

Times like this, I was glad Miss Mary Mack was meticulously picky with who she liked and didn't like because I didn't want to bring just any dog home. I wanted it to be one who Mary got along with but still felt like Luz's choice.

With Luz distracted and all this pet adoption stuff, the last thing on her mind was bringing up this whole proposal fallout. If we never brought it up again, even that would be too soon.

Parking in the nearby empty parking lot, I got out to make sure Luz didn't need any help getting Mary out of the car. The second that door opened, Mary hopped out, jumping excitedly toward me like she was on her way to Disneyland.

Who knows? Maybe this was Disneyland for her. She, unlike Luz, was excited to spend the rest of her days with a ready and willing soulmate. "Here, Miss Mary Mack, let's get you on a lease before these boys be thinking you're in desperate need of *anybody*," Luz said, securing her leash.

Luz surprised me when she took my hand, leading me to the shelter's front entrance. On Luz's insistence, we were early for our appointment. I'd already had an idea of the process being a long-time dog owner, so since everything was new for her, I let her fill out the paperwork and do the all talking when it came to growing our dog family. In time, we were finally joined by the attendant who would be our guide to the shelter.

"Hi, it's nice to meet you both. I'm Sarah. Was it a long trip for you?" Her kind eyes creased at the corners, flashing a warm smile.

Luz had set her eyes on adopting from a female and Black-owned animal shelter, so while it was further than some great places closer to us, it was her first time and I wanted it to be memorable.

"Eh, not too long. We're just inside the city." I warmly replied.

"Yeah, your wife was telling me over the phone that she wasn't sure any Black-owned shelters existed, so thanks for driving up to see us. That means a lot when you could have gone someplace closer." Her cringy comment left a weird taste in my mouth, forcing a knee-jerk reaction to correct her.

"Oh, she's not my wife. She's just my girlfriend." The comment causing both the attendant and Luz to enter in an awkward bout of silence. It wasn't long before Luz wore that look on her face that told me the minute she got me alone, she *was* going to address it.

"Um, why don't we just get started?" Sarah's hazel eyes widened as she turned on the balls of her feet to start the beginning of the tour.

"I love that you guys have a cane corso. What I know about

those dogs is that they like to be the boss. You're gonna want a strong dog like her and because of their temperament, they don't always get along with every breed. The best part about it, though, is your angel can give birth up until her last days, which I'm sure you knew. The hardest part is finding her the right mate."

Due to her breed and availability, I knew finding another cane corso wasn't possible unless we were willing to shop around for people who bred them. My experience, however, had convinced me a labrador, doberman, or even a pitbull could still work, so I was prepared for anything so long as Mary and them had good chemistry.

"So, I'm actually not as knowledgeable as my, ahem, *boyfriend* when it comes to compatibility and all that good stuff. Are there any breeds you'd recommend?"

"What can you tell me about her behavior?"

"She's pretty independent, but the idea was for her to get along with a breed past the mating season. A breed that can keep up with her and ease her loneliness and anxiety when we take long trips and stuff."

Not gonna lie, I was really unsure of what long trips she was speaking of, considering neither one of us decided whether our winter trip was going to be happening this year. I nodded in agreement to fake a united front.

"Why don't you guys just take a look around? Your angel will weed out any dog she doesn't have chemistry with. Then when you need some help, just give me a holler. I find that most adoptees do better when I'm not hovering."

In all honesty, I think Sarah was just trying to find a way out to give us space, sensing the tension. Bringing my emotions in check, I thanked her and told her we'd take her up on her offer to let us explore on our own. Making our way through the kennel area, Luz broke her silence to challenge the remark I made earlier.

"So, just your girlfriend, huh? That's an interesting way to describe me."

"It's also a true way to describe you," I retorted, preparing myself for anything when Luz did that scary thing with her mouth at the beginning of any argument.

"You know what? Let me calm myself, cuz I know these animals are feeding off our negative energy and this day is supposed to be about Mary. Our drama can wait." She faked a smile, but I knew that wouldn't be the end of it.

Especially with the hour and a half car ride we had getting back. Letting Mary lead the way, Luz walked by a series of cages, all containing different breeds of dogs that could be either a hit or miss. A beagle mix barked to grab our attention, and despite Mary not being much of a defensive dog, she hoofed back, prompting Luz to offer some feminine advice.

"Yeah, that's right, Mary. U.N.I.T.Y. Don't be letting that beagle call you a bitch," she encouraged before going full on dog-mom mode. "Look at all these eligible bachelors. You have so many options."

If I weren't so irritated with her right now, I would have burst out laughing. Being such a proud man, I knew needing space was a commitment, so laughing at the joke would have lead her to believe things were fine between us and they weren't.

Stopping to engage with a golden retriever mix, I bent down and he went to lick my hand. He reminded me of one of the dogs I had growing up and, if it wasn't for all the hair they left behind, I would have argued to get a retriever.

Then again, I'd taken a chance on Mary and it had worked out. Dogs like retrievers were easy, predictable. If only woman worked the same way. Before I realized it, Luz had already pulled back Sarah, our former attendant, with a legion of overwhelming first timer questions.

"There was this one I wanted to get a closer look at. He was the only one Miss Mary Mack didn't growl at. I believe he's the one at the end. Um...I think it looks like a rottweiler but I'm not good with breeds and stuff. All I know is that he's black and brown."

"Great. I'll give you a closer look."

Grabbing Luz's arm, I took her to the side, leaving us steps behind the staff member helping us. "Luz, don't get attached to just any dog because Mary didn't have a bad reaction. It's important to consider the dog's health history, medical conditions. The reason why he's in the shelter in the first place. Not saying you're doing it wrong. I just know how you get. You fall in love with the first one you like without exploring other options."

Eyeing me up and down, she did that intimidating thing she did with her neck. As many times as I've tried to imitate it, it was damn near impossible as a man. "Well, lucky for you. If I wasn't the type to fall for the first face I saw, you and I might not even be here."

With that, she shook her curly fro, lifted her chin, turned her back to me, and sashayed in the opposite direction. I hated how right she was, but I hated myself more for giving her the ammunition. Let's see this damn dog.

"So, this fella here is a rottweiler/lab mix," Sarah said as she eased the keys inside the lock and opened up the cage. "We call him Melo as we don't refer to them as their previous names, but they adapt well when and if you rename them," she finished warmly.

"Why do you call him Melo?"

"It's so silly. Truth is, you put a ball in front of him and he always wants to play with it. It's more like a nod to Carmelo Anthony. But for a rottweiler mix, his temperament isn't as bad."

Okay, so the dog likes basketball. Doesn't mean he's the one we should go with. With a gentle calmness, Melo walked up to Luz, greeting her face with happy licks and wet kisses. She turned to me, her lips forming into a pout, as her eyes narrowed softly.

"Evan," she whined, doing exactly what I warned her not to do. He wasn't even that cute.

"Baby, come on. You said you wouldn't get attached right away. You haven't even given any one else a chance." But before I could finish, Melo tiptoed over to me, all sweet and friendly with his tongue out, and his soulful marble eyes. He was trying hard to get me to bend down and pet him.

"Fuck, what was I saying?" Okay, so maybe he was a *little* cute. But if I was trying to show Luz how to make a better judgment call, I sure was bad at it any time someone with four legs came around.

"Is it normal to have chemistry with the first dog you take out?" Luz questioned as she loosened Mary's leash and Mary strolled over for what I assumed would be a fight for my attention. Mary was normally jealous, protective, and *very* vocal about it. To my surprise, she just nuzzled him away just so they can engage in a little excitement contest for who could leap the highest.

I'd never seen Mary interact with another adult dog like that. Call me shocked. "Normally, it varies. Especially when a dog has had multiple owners. But the right match finds you or at least that's what I think," Sarah said bashfully, lowering her head.

Luz bent down a second time, taking Mary's face in her hands and playing with the ticklish spot behind her ears. "You sure about him, girl?" Mary's indication for yes was usually a lick on the mouth, and I couldn't help laughing to myself. I never thought I'd get used to Luz normalizing dog kisses.

"I think we have our answer. Let's get the process started."

What usually took me minutes took Luz an hour when it came to the paperwork. She always had questions. Not that there was ever such a thing as too many questions, but in my effort to make her feel involved, I let her take the lead.

That and I hoped she'd be too tired to talk on the way back home. Like a lot of shit, I was wrong. Sitting in the front seat this time, she waited until I merged onto the freeway to start the conversation I'd been dreading all day.

"So, where did you go last night?" She lowered the music and turned to face me.

"Look, I'm sorry I walked out last night. I just needed time to myself to think. It's hard to do that when you live with someone. I'm sorry if I worried you. I just..." Hesitating because I didn't like the idea that what I wanted to say would hurt her feelings.

"You wouldn't have gotten much out of me last night," I admitted. Checking into a hotel hadn't been my proudest moment, but the plan wasn't to go too far just in case something bad had happened.

"I just got a room at that place on 31st Street. The one we pass all the time when we go to that sushi spot."

"You're right. I was worried. I wasn't even sure we were still doing this today."

"Well, it takes some effort to adopt the dog and I know we didn't have time to waste, so..." Speeding up to pass an old guy doing forty-five miles per hour, I cursed under my breath when he stuck his middle finger up at me to witness through my rearview mirror. Vermont plates. Fucking figures.

"Evan, I've been wanting to bring this up for days, but every time I try and talk to you, you shut down. In a very Luz sort-of-fashion as you put it in the past, might I add." Throwing my past words against me.

"You and I process things differently, Luz. I don't like the idea of blowing up on you just because I'm angry. Nothing gets resolved when you're angry."

Luz let out a deep sigh, proceeding on to finish what she had to say. "Yeah, I know. It's just we haven't been the same since our anniversary. You don't want to talk, and I can't get you to talk. Sometimes it feels like the only thing that would get you to open up is if we went on one of those couples" retreats." At the mere suggestion, I took my gaze away from the road long enough to shoot her an incredulous look. She had to be out of her mind.

"Papi. I know what you're thinking."

"Okay, so if you already know, then there's no need to say it." I abhorred anything that had to do with putting our business as a couple out there. That meant steering conversations away when someone asked a personal question regarding the state of our relationship. That meant limiting social media posts, which wasn't hard for me since I wasn't good at it as she was. However, none of those things were even remotely close to what she was suggesting.

Was she really trying to convince me that couples" therapy was our only answer? The idea of trauma bonding with a bunch of strangers was something I knew she had to have only suggested as a joke. So, why the hell was she looking so serious?

"Evan, you've been so distant, and I'll be real. That makes me hella insecure. I think if we could just be open and try it, it'd be a great way for us to figure some stuff out and help clear the air."

"You don't want to get married. I do. What's not clear about that?" I asked, looking away from the road again, long enough to measure her vacant reaction. "Luz. You know how I feel about that. Discussing our problems in front of strangers. In an Italian home, you kept things private. You got everything off your chest at confessional. Which reminds me. I'm right about due for one."

Luz threw up her hands in defeat, releasing an impatient snare. "Urgh. It's clear you're not taking this seriously. I know it's not a cultural norm for you, but it's not one for me either, but if I had let that stop me years ago, I would have been forever living in trauma. Black folk aren't exactly known for lining up in droves to seek therapy, and it's worse when your parents aren't American.

"You have to plan five escape routes just in case someone who knows *one* person your mom might know, and you have to hide why you're even there in the first place. You using the Italian card is not a valid enough excuse." *Did she just say the Italian card?* She was lucky I was driving.

"Let's say I entertain this idea. There's no way I'd go where people know knew me—"

"Even better. The one I was considering was a week retreat in Idyllwild-Pine Cone, California," she interrupted.

"California? Two weeks? If we do something like that, it's going to cut into our winter vacation time. I thought we were talking about the French Riviera? Or Rome?"

Luz rolled her eyes for what felt like the third time this conversation. "You are not understanding me. If we don't get our shit figured out, we won't have another chance to go to Rome or the French Riviera. ¿Me entiendes?" Her comment forced me to let go of a heavy sigh. I couldn't believe I was admitting this, but she was right. We had to address this issue at some point.

"I'm telling you what therapy has done for me. Can we at least see what it can do for us?" Fighting the urge to be argumentative, it dawned on me that if she would go through all this trouble to work through our problems, she must have really seen a future with me. For that, I figured I could be more open minded.

"Are you absolutely sure about this?" I asked one final time, certain I would never be truly satisfied with her answer.

"No, but I'm sure about you. And I'm sure about me. I just want to try it. I think we're worth at least that much," her voice lowered to a husked tone.

To ease her insecurity, I took her hand and planted a kiss on her wrist. "Okay."

CHAPTER SEVEN

Evan

My trip to the bathroom took way more time than I anticipated. The luxury business first class lounge had been modest, but the men's room had a line out the door that made me regret having so much coffee a half hour before we were meant to board.

I would be lying if I said the extra time to myself wasn't nice. My mind was still racing at the thought of going halfway across the country to attend a couples" retreat at the last minute. To be honest, the idea of *individual* therapy had never bothered me. In fact, after seeing the personal development it got out of Luz, at times I had considered it myself just to see if it would help me become a better partner.

It was the idea of *couples"* therapy that put me in defense mode. For most of my life, I had always thought that relationships were sacred and no one should be in your business but you and your partner. It was why when Luz and I didn't see eye-to-eye, I didn't go running to family or friends. When it came to our families, at least I could say that if we ever became in-laws, we wouldn't be entering a marriage with negativity, gossip, or animosity.

That was if we ever made it that far.

Luz had always been a modern woman, but it still shocked the shit out of me that she hadn't even been *considering* marriage from the time that we got back together. Not even when we started living together, either. I knew not *every* woman wanted to get married, I just didn't know that *my* woman wouldn't want to get married. The thought made rounds in my head and I still didn't believe it.

By the time I returned to the business first class lounge, Luz was adorably bouncing up and down, waiting at the entrance, worried I wouldn't make it in time.

"I tried to call you but I forgot your phone was in my carry on." She transferred my suitcase back to me after guarding our luggage.

"The line was long and I was trying to avoid using the plane's bathroom," I said in a hurried huff after we rushed to reach the boarding area of our plane.

Lucky for us, they were still boarding first class, so our wait was minimal as we made it to our seats. This was something new for her, but Luz picked the window seat, challenging her fear of looking out the window during a flight.

Without needing to be told, I silently volunteered to place our luggage in the overhead compartment. Luz had placed the carry on under my seat, so when I sat down, there wasn't much to do before take-off. Since it'd be another twenty minutes before the plane's departure, it seemed like a good time as any to see if Luz was okay.

"Everything okay?" For as long as I have known Luz, I'd known that flying was her least favorite way to travel. She understood that for certain destinations it was necessary, but when it wasn't, she wasn't shy about her preference for trains and driving.

Her panic attacks were understandable. I had never lost a parent, so while I empathized, it was on a long list of things Luz had more experience with. It had to be devastating that the last image you had of a lost loved one was through a tragedy. When it came to making her feel at peace with flying, it was my job to check in and make sure she wasn't internally freaking out.

Her knuckles turned pale, digging them into the armrests, suggesting that it was the best time to help her steady her breathing. "You know how nervous I get right before take-off. I just need a minute, I'm sure it'll pass," she dismissed.

"I'll help you. Just remember what we practiced."

When Luz and I had shared our first *official* vacation together, it had taken me close to two hours to ease her anxiety once the plane took off. It required researching a ton of breathing techniques and methods to calm the nerves that I was proud to say now it only taken ten to twenty minutes to get the same result. I'm sure it was because she trusted me. Nonetheless, after departure, I was able to calm her in a record breaking nine minutes, prompting me to order a movie since we had plenty of time to kill.

"So, there's *Who Framed Roger Rabbit? Despicable Me? Wreck-It Ralph?* There's also *The Incredible Spider Man.* You said you liked Andrew Garfield's Spiderman, right?" Weighing out all our options. After confirming that her forever Spiderman was Miles Morales and if he wasn't in it, she didn't want it, she pushed for me to find something we could both agree on.

"They have *The Godfather*—"

"Put on *Wreck-It Ralph*," she interrupted, knowing that once I watched *The Godfather*, I'd be quoting it our entire trip. It wasn't the most positive Italian-American portrayal, but it was hard to argue with the fact it was the most well-known. I could watch that series a thousand times before I ever got tired of them, which was an interest Luz and I did not share.

Believe it or not, times like this were when I was the most at peace. Sure, I loved the night out, but sitting down and enjoying something as simple as watching a movie together were the moments that I lived for. The moments that I wanted to share with the person I grew old with. I wanted that woman to be Luz. I mean, we were already so good at it.

Luz introduced me to tons of movies and shows I probably would've never watched without her influence, so it tripped me out that despite her taste in animated whimsical movies, she never thought about what it would be like sharing that with a family.

Like always, *Wreck-It Ralph* was an entertaining movie about a guy who created his own problems but everything worked out in the end. I was strangely confused by the movie's conclusion, wondering if changing the way I looked at what I really wanted might solve my problems.

As we watched the credits conclude the movie, I suggested Luz get some sleep, surprised to be met with reluctance. "I'm still a little anxious. I don't think I could sleep based on my nerves," she spoke in a sleepy tone.

"We could watch *The Godfather*," I suggested. "I'm sure that would put you right to sleep," getting lost in her heavy eyes.

"Did you remember to pack that vibrator?" she asked in a pout that screamed both innocence and devious at the same time.

"Here? Right now?" Unsure whether the excitement was obvious in my tone. When she confirmed with a nod, I found myself pulling back the drape that doubled as a Do Not Disturb signal for the stewardess walking by.

I hadn't forgotten to pack it, I just didn't think we would need it. All our issues just took me out of a fucking kind of mood, and plus Luz and I were technically already part of the Mile-High Club. But it *was* the first time I'd used a vibrator on her while flying.

Bending over to retrieve the partly charged toy, I whispered that we should put it on at its lowest setting and play our movie without headphones to drown out some of the noise. My instinct was to put on *Despicable Me*, but after Luz argued that there was no way she wanted to climax with that in the background, *The*

Godfather it was. Mental note: if I wanted her to watch *The Godfather*, offer orgasms before, during, or after.

Lifting up the adjustable armrests that separated us, I leaned into kiss her, knowing she would need a little bit more warming up. Her lips were light, yet sweet with remnants of the gourmet apple tart she had ordered at the lounge.

Strangely, the soothing scents reminded me of autumn, leaving behind hints of cinnamon and sugared pie crust. As we attempted to keep our breathing at a respectable whisper, I kept most of my petting above the belt. That was, until my hand traveled down to make sure it could easily slide into her waistband.

Invited by warmth, wetness, and her inviting lips, I smoothed two fingers in front of her opening, knowing I had next to no self-control when it came to a horny Luz.

Our lips melded together, fighting for control until she pulled away long enough to provide further instructions.

"Do it now." To preserve the battery I hadn't turned it on until it was time to play. Luz squirmed upon the initial contact, but had thankfully eased up and relaxed into the sensations. "I'm just not used to not being able to moan as loud as I want."

With that out of the way, I gently moved the vibrating toy up and down, massaging her folds, reveling in the fact that my fingers were joining in and getting lost in her slickness. Times like this, I *really* wish that I could eat her pussy. She probably tasted so right good now, her walls tensing, gushing out juices that were making my mouth water.

Despite her thighs being spread as wide as her clothes and positioning would allow, I could tell that she wished that she could be stretched out on a bed somewhere. Her fingers dug into the forearm of the arm controlling the toy, as she breathlessly leaned into kiss me, frustrated that she couldn't moan at the volume necessary to communicate how good it felt.

The tension in her upper body would've been an on-brand sign for her, had she not unexpectedly bit my lower lip before pulling away to rest in her pleasure. Short, repetitive, gathered breaths followed her release of tension as rhythmic spasms pulsed against my hand and the toy.

"Shit," she spoke through a combination of a strain and a whisper, as I found a travel pack of baby wipes and gave my hands and the toy a quick swipe. "Mmm...I think that helped," she moaned into my mouth leaning in for a kiss.

"I could use a nap if you didn't mind." She yawned, giving me a temporary sense of pride knowing I was partially the reason for her current fatigue.

"Go ahead," I assured her and my hope was that she'd sleep for most of the flight. A flicker of shame came over me admitting to myself that I'd rather do anything but talk right now, but an even bigger sense of relief knowing now I wouldn't have to.

CHAPTER EIGHT

Luz

Light taps to my shoulder nudged me awake as it took me a minute to come to. I always dreaded waking up from my fantasy dream of being chosen as the next Avatar. Couldn't a plane ride have taken a bit longer? I was just about to be ordained, damn.

"Luz," Evan whispered, his normally soft eyes appearing piercing considering it was my first image awake.

"They're about to let first class unboard, you got to get up." Keeping his voice low and hushed.

"Are we in California already?" I asked with an unexpected snort, a sure sign of my disorientation. My confirmation that we had landed came in as notification through the pilot thanking us for flying with their airlines over the loud speaker.

It didn't matter whether I was alone on this, but knowing we'd landed safe, I took a moment to raise to my feet and clap. It was definitely a Dominican thing, but I clapped *every* time a plane landed. I was so grateful to be on land again.

Once I got my bearings, I grabbed the carry-on bag under Evan's seat, as he reached up to grab our suitcases in the overhead compartment. Ensuring that we left nothing behind, now that I was more alert, the color underneath Evan's eyes looked like he hadn't slept the whole plane right here.

He wasn't moving like a zombie, but he was sluggish every step of the way to the departure gate. Normally I had to put more pep in my step to meet his long stride, especially with heels on, but right now he seemed like a shell of himself. This would give me a chance to offer to drive. As someone who had only had her license a whole year, I was always happy to get behind the wheel. Nearby conversations, delay announcements, and large digital monitors displaying arrival and departure times made this a typical airport experience but LAX wasn't as big as I thought it would be. I don't know why I was expecting something fancier.

It took a few minutes of walking to finally feel the cricks in my neck from having such an awkward nap that I was tempted to hit up one of the gift shops on the way to the car rental station to see if they had a neck kneading massager to loosen some of the tension.

"Urgh, I just *hate* walking past the food court," I whined, knowing damn well I'd eaten before the plane ride. I was failing miserably at blocking out the smell of cinnamon rolls, Chinese food, and pizza. As a native New Yorker, I'd leave that pizza to the East Coast, but a cinnamon bun sounded nice right about now. Gosh, why was Evan ignoring all this?

"Let me know if you want coffee or a quick bite to eat." Dangling the option to see if he would fold.

"We don't know how busy the car rental place will be. Let's just do that first and then we can get food."

It was a fifteen-minute power walk to reach the car rental stations. By the looks of things, business was steady. Evan was worried for nothing though, as we were in and out within ten minutes.

Evan had chosen a modest hybrid SUV, similar to his car back home, so the drive from the airport to Idyllwild-Pine Cone would be a breeze once I started tinkering with the car's navigational system.

On instinct, Evan took the driver's side before I could claim it, so I went from sitting on a plane to sitting in the passenger's seat. Guess I'll just play with my phone.

"I'm just remembering that I can now use my phone. I wonder if I should text Mikayla to see if we can hang out. She's been booked and busy ever since she moved to LA I'm sure if I asked, she'd be willing to meet up and maybe even host us before we head back home."

You would never believe my cousin Mikayla and I had had a strained relationship growing up with how close we were now. While I would have loved if she had stayed on the East Coast so we could've hung out more, I was happy knowing she was out here trying new things and being in places that challenged her comfort zone.

"You know LA isn't a hop skip and jump away from Idyllwild-Pine Cone, right?" His voice strained and throaty despite smiling through it.

"Yeah, but maybe she'd be willing to drive and meet us that halfway—"

"Luz, don't forget why we're here. Catching up with family is nice, but we're not exactly here on vacation." His tone ending with some unresolved tension in his voice. As we were approaching the retreat, my guess was he had just as much anxiety flaring up as I did, expressing it in his own confusing way.

He had a point though: if this were another California trip, visiting family would have been a great idea. On this trip, not so much. Aside from the 2000s Alternative Rock playing in the background, the ride was pretty peaceful. My nerves made me more talkative than normal, so you can imagine how torturing it was to sit in a quiet car when I wanted nothing more than to drown out the sereneness with some hype music to turn my brain off.

Turns out I didn't have to. Thirty minutes into driving, Evan kept noticeably rubbing his eyes, giving me something new to focus on.

"Babe, are you okay?"

"Yeah, I just...I think I should have taken you up on that offer to stop for coffee. I have like, no energy," he confessed.

"Did you get any sleep on the plane?" He confirmed that he hadn't just in case I woke up in the middle of my sleep and required talking down. He looked awful.

"Maybe you should just stretch out in the back and take a breather." He rubbed his face, before admitting he could use the break. Pulling over, I stepped out of the passenger side seat and had Evan pop open the trunk, so I could trade my pumps for flats.

Evan climbed into the backseat, stretching out as much as his tall frame would allow, as I handed him the crappy airplane pillow that I had used during our flight.

"I just need twenty minutes and I'll be as good as new," he boldly stated but by the time I revved up the engine, his gentle snores echoed throughout the car.

He was going to be passed out for a while, so it was going to be an entire car ride where no one would keep me company. Now that he was asleep, I thought about calling Mikayla and if we kept our voices low enough, he'd stay asleep the rest of the ride.

Pulling into a McDonald's driveway, I retrieved my Bluetooth AirPods from my carry on and placed my phone in the portable hands-free-holder, then tapped the screen to bring up Siri.

"Siri, FaceTime Mikayla." Commanding my app, hoping this was one way to cure my driving loneliness. Within seconds, Mikayla's face covered my phone screen, as I apologized that because I was driving, the angle would feel off.

"I'm so happy you made it to California safe," she dragged out, sounding like a valley girl.

"You over here sounding like Hilary Banks. Dark skinned Hillary by the way, not the light skinned one," I teased, prompting her to fake her laughter on the other end.

"You'll have to forgive me if I can't turn up. There is currently a sleeping passenger that I don't want to wake." Gesturing toward the backseat. Mikayla nodded, acknowledging that she wouldn't be too loud, which wasn't a stretch for her but hard as hell for me.

"So, have you gotten to see much of California so far? Tell me you got to see your first palm tree," she said in her usual coy manner.

"All I've really seen are freeways so far, but I know in an hour or so I'm gonna see a lot more cedar and oak." Referring to where the site the retreat was being held. "I was actually just talking about you. We planned for a week since that's how long the retreat is but since we're using this as our winter vacay, we took off two to see California. Do you think you'd want to meet up after?" Mikayla laughed, like I'd said the funniest thing, making me regret suggesting it.

"Girl, if you feel like driving far. Everything out here you have to drive an hour and a half to get to. It is *not* like taking the 6 from the Bronx to Manhattan."

Having never been to California, Mikayla explained how California had a lot more tolls than New York, and all the other small things she'd had close to two years to get used to. Legal U-turns, next-to-no humidity type summers, and alcohol at a Walgreens were things I could certainly get used to if I weren't so attached to NYC.

Our conversation had definitely put me in a better mood, so good I was disappointed when she excused herself to answer the door for her take out. She insisted on keeping me on the phone, but wanting her to enjoy her food, I let her go. It was times like this I wish I could call Candice. Due to a last-minute business trip to Rio, she was in knee deep work mode with a client and while I was tempted to check in with Genevieve to tell her that I had taken her advice, the time difference was too great and I was sure she was getting ready for bed. Not wanting to disturb Evan, I decided that while I was on my own, I might as well just let the beautiful Mother Nature entertain me.

CHAPTER NINE

Luz

One of the many things I struggled to get used to as a city girl, was the call back to nature. The drive to Idyllwild-Pine Cone was *anything* but the city. Gone were the images of asphalt and buildings and replaced with the sight of wilderness and everything Mother Nature intended her beautiful creation to be.

Evan would have loved all the subtle changes to the larger than life trees, the sight of wild berries growing, and the meandering trails left for those who loved the outdoors. Given how fast he had fallen asleep, and how little time I gave myself to appreciate the great outdoors, I decided this gem could be just for me.

Dating Evan, I was still getting used to all the interests he had, or at least had grown up doing that I had chalked up as privileged shit. Growing up comfortable middle class, things like camping and kayaking were just obvious when it came to family vacation activities, but when you grew up below the poverty line, the only place we ever "vacationed" to was where my family was from in the DR. One hundred percent of the time it was to visit relatives.

Looking back, it was definitely seeing this shit. Growing up in the part of the United States that I did, I never truly appreciated the simple life my mom had back on the island until now. Our first summer together, Evan had surprised me with a road trip to Lake George.

It hadn't been a perfect trip; upon renting a kayak to explore all that Lake George had to offer, the steering tail to our boat broke and it took us hours to navigate back to the rental site once we were miles out in the middle of nowhere. In fact, if we hadn't met some Irish guy floating out three hours into getting lost, we would have never made it back. My entire body ached from having to paddle back, as Evan had to hold on to the back of it to make sure the boat went in the direction of the way I needed the paddle to go, but I couldn't help thinking that if we hadn't been dating I would have never had such an interesting White-shit-I-aint-never-gonna-do-again story come time for the holidays.

There had been a lot of things I had never been open to that with Evan, I now did on instinct. If you had told me a year and a half ago that this Black Dominicana would be making homemade pasta sauce from scratch, I would have lost a bet.

I wasn't one with nature, but I certainly had a better relation-ship with the quiet crisp, great outdoors because of Evan. I just hope that this retreat would help us figure our shit out.

***

The purring engine finally came to a calm when I found a good spot in the parking lot. I was really going to have to consider a getting my own hybrid SUV when we got back home because up until today, I never thought a car this spacious could be this quiet.

Not wanting to wake Evan, I considered checking in and making sure all our bags got in okay while he was still enjoying his nap, but he never gave me the chance. By the time I opened the trunk, he was right by my side, taking on the bigger suitcase

Aside from a low mummer consisting of "Let me help you with that," he wasn't very chatty, but I'm sure he was in a hurry to get to our accommodation so his nap could be continued. At this point, I didn't blame him but knowing he was probably going to fall back asleep meant we would have less time to discuss what our expectations were with the retreat.

We hadn't discussed it as often as I would've liked to, despite our last-minute decision to attend, but I was grateful he even *wanted* to come. I was looking forward to have a real one-on-one so that I wouldn't have to constantly guess what was on his mind.

Researching the host of the retreat, outside of him being a YuVuber, he was right up my alley when it came to the stuff that he discussed on his channel.

While my degree had led me down the path of journalism, he'd let his study in human sexuality lead him to become a sex therapist that focused on intimacy. I was drawn in by Genevieve's pitch, but I had to say, his colorful interests secured his bag.

Dr. Vinh Nguyen. PhD. Sex educator. Daddy Dominant. Past that, I didn't even get far on his About Me page. I wasn't well versed in the kink community, so it didn't surprise me that I had never heard of him. His mission statements were impressive, though.

Give him a week and he could help couples bring out the best in themselves. No promises that your best will be right for your current partner but through relearning and recreating intimacy in one's relationship, you were guaranteed to learn if your relation ship was even worth saving. I couldn't speak for Evan, but I felt like ours was. So, the hope was that this fricking intimacy doctor would help as promised.

After handing the car keys to Evan for safekeeping, we made our way to the lodging check in area to confirm that we were in the right place. Neither of us had been to a couples' retreat before, so it was starting to look like the vacation spot we deserved, than an opportunity to reclaim the honeymoon stages of one's relationship.

"Cattaneo and De Los Santos?" Evan confirmed with the concierge about our reservation.

"Ah yes, you're with the retreat group. Just give me a moment to ensure your room is prepared," as the pepper-haired White woman picked up the phone and quickly hung up.

It felt a little jarring how she'd picked up a walkie talkie to confirm our arrival, but it all made sense by the time we were being handed the keys to our room.

An unfamiliar-familiar face approached.

"Luz and Evan?" Like a good neighbor, Dr. Vinh Nguyen was there. This dude must want this money.

"You must be Dr. Vinh Nguyen," Evan outstretched a hand to him, before he assured that we could just call him Vinh.

Much like Evan, he was tall or at least noticeably so when you were five-eight.

He was *really* handsome in person, the whole flight here I kept thinking about how no person could look *that* much like their website photos in real life. Vinh was that and then some while still managing to keep a professional air about him upon meeting guests for the first time.

"I'm sure you're wondering why I'm here. Typically for new couples, I like to introduce myself and explain a little bit about the seminar and programs." According to Vinh, he hosted 6-10 of these retreats a year, all ranging from a weekend to a three-week timespan. I was feeling some kinda way that he mentioned one or two were held in the Caribbean. Hell, we could have booked one of those.

Couples were a lot more open to discussing their problems when they weren't in comfortable environments like home, where they were close to people that they thought might easily judge them for seeking counseling. Worst case scenario couples may not reach the root of their issue, but there were all these self-care activities to encourage individuals to bring home with them to work on themselves, too. He clearly had a Mind-Body-Soul approach to therapy, something I'm sure Evan and I were pretty lacking in.

"Let me know if you guys would like any help with your luggage? Or need guidance understanding the programs and schedule—"

"Thank you, but we're good," Evan politely declined. Unsure of whether Vinh could read body language, I hoped he couldn't tell the expression Evan wore was him being courteous, but still harboring reluctance. Maybe that wasn't fair; I knew he was still tired and was just trying to get to that room so he could pass out.

"Before I go, I just wanted to encourage you to attend our icebreaker dinner. If you're changing time zones and looking to get rest, I won't keep you but you're one of the three couples who has never attended one before. I find that groups run more efficient when participants meet beforehand."

Evan nodded as he shot a quick "We'll see," before bidding Vinh the grace to move on before we rolled our luggage to our reserved cabin.

"That was weird." Evan finally breaking the silence after saying so little when we had the face-to-face with Dr. Vinh Nguyen.

"What was so weird about it?" I asked, hoping to pick his brain.

"It seemed *implied* that we're expected to attend this thing more than once," Evan stated frustratingly confused.

"I'm pretty sure not all couples do." Taking the room key out of my pocket and ushering the door open. "Couples' counseling isn't a seven-day old magic trick, it takes work. Which is why I'm sure couples come back. All well-oiled machines require maintenance." I said, trying to sound reassuring.

That didn't go over as smooth as I thought, because for as

tired as Evan looked, frustration joined the myriad of emotions Evan was wearing through his features. He rubbed his face, knowing it would do little to hide his furrowed eyebrows and sullen eyes, but attempted to nonetheless.

"Obviously, my hope is that we'll be one of the couples Dr. Nguyen never has to see again." I said, trying to lighten my voice to sound more cherry and hopeful. Evan didn't even bother unpacking his suitcase, as he slipped off his shoes and collapsed on the bed.

"You're being uncomfortably quiet," I admitted, knowing he hadn't fallen asleep yet but hoping he'd admit something revealing before he was no longer conscious.

"Luz, I'm just processing. It's still a lot to take in." He brought his long legs to the middle of the bed.

Knowing he needed reassuring, I reminded him of all the benefits therapy was currently giving me and most of my family. "Just remember that infamous Thanksgiving. Not all therapy is productive but when it came to my family, it provided a fucking miracle."

After my Aunt Noelia and I read one another, nearly all my aunts considered getting therapy. My uncle had been too proud and thought it was clearly a woman problem, but those of my family members that did follow through were finally on some path to healing.

It felt like I was in an alternative universe when Aunt Noelia invited me to one of her sessions, so that we could clear some of the animosity that festered between us outside of her resentment of me.

I learned that her frustration with me had been rooted in her inability to relate since she was from a generation of women who lived to please everyone around them, especially their parents. Even I had to take a step back and ask was I indirectly shaming her by making her feel like the choices she made in life weren't progressive enough. Our tension wasn't absolved overnight, but the fact that we had gotten that far was because of therapy.

"I just want us to be better. Or at least come from a better place of understanding each other." I slipped out of my shoes and decided Evan was too tired for me to be keeping him up to reassure me right now.

If anything, he'd fall asleep, and then I'd just get upset that he hadn't heard anything, so it was best to wait until he'd gotten the proper rest. Maybe it was time to explore the rustic outline of the room.

For a retreat location, it was in good taste. The walls at least gave off the impression that it was made entirely by wood while still being able to ensure central air conditioning. If this had been an actual vacation, Evan would totally pick a room like this for a camping trip. It almost looked like everything was built right into the woods.

The bathroom was the golden triangle, because the lighting and floor panel work was to die for. I hadn't really needed a shower, but the self-care aspect of it forced my hand. All the complimentary shower oils and soaps made it that much easier to indulge.

The alone time was nice, the shower soothing the tension in my shoulders and back, relaxing me into the idea of joining the icebreaker festivities in just a few hours' time. All I could remember about what Vinh shared that stuck with me was we would get to see a handful of couples at different stages in their lives and relationships.

Despite meeting each other in our teens, I really hoped that Evan and I weren't the only couple who had been together as adults for less than two years. Not that it should matter. Everyone was here for the same thing, whether they were seasoned or in the honeymoon stage like us. After settling into a tank top and some undergarments, I sat down to study the week's full program, as not everything had been listed on the website.

For seven days, there was a lot to do. There were even activities you could choose to do, depending if a couple required alone time, which was to work together and communicate not just to venture off to have sex. Evan and I disagreed with a lot of things, but we had agreed on this. I was confident that all we needed was some guidance on how to communicate better and we'd be good as new.

CHAPTER TEN

Luz

"Luz, would you *please* just go with the first one you had on?" Evan questioningly scolding me from the bed, visibly annoyed. I swear, ever since he woke up, he'd been such a crab. Maybe if he had gotten some pussy, he wouldn't be so damn wound up.

Technically we were on a retreat, so I'm sure no one would care what I wore, but we had sacrificed our winter vacation for this. *Someone* was going to see me in my vacation digs. "Should I wear my hair up or down?" Debating it, as I modeled the difference in the mirror to judge the options for myself. My instinct was to wear it down but I eventually decided to go for an updo consisting of two curly Afro puffs before finishing off the look with the flowers that had been on display in the room. They were going to die anyway, so they might as well help me look cute in the process.

Evan finally arose from bed and met my reflection in the mirror, hooking one arm around my shoulder and the other one around my arm clasping both hands to hold me. "Luz, you look pretty enough." Resting his chin on my shoulder, looking straight into the mirror to show his face of frustration. "Can we just go?"

"This coming from a man who didn't even want to go? Why are you so worried about the schedule all of a sudden? The icebreaker dinner, in addition to some of the other activities were optional," I stated firmly, praying he didn't smudge my eye makeup.

"You're the one who wanted me to come here." His wild green eyes widened, almost as if to silently scold me. "There will be no activity skipping whatsoever. I just didn't want to be the last couple walking in, having everyone staring and judging us like we're not taking this seriously," he ended in a jovial tone, before admitting if we were the last couple to show up, he was totally going to throw me under the bus.

Evan appeared twice as annoyed as before when I eventually went with the first outfit of the three I had already tried on, prompting us to be a few minutes late than the dinner's start time. Add in the time it took for us to walk and find the carriage house and we were close to ten minutes late. Let's hope Vinh was running on people of color time, because I was certainly running on Black girl time today.

As we made our way over to the corridor, it wasn't long before we were met with a cozy rustic entranceway leading straight to the carriage house. Much like everything around here, it gave off a gentle woodsy feel, as if the forest and spa were extensions of each other. People were already engaging in conversation by the time we arrived, instantly making me regret that we had wasted proper icebreaker time just for me to look fly.

One positive note: at least I looked fly.

"Well, if it isn't the newlyweds," an older White man joked under his breath.

"I guess the lovebirds finally decided to make an appearance," with what appeared to be his wife finishing up.

Apparently, everyone had been making bets to whether we were newly married or not. As far as it looked to them, we were spending every waking moment to fill with a quickie and last-minute head. Heh, if only that were true...

"Can't think of a better reason to show up late," a younger queer woman joked with her older wife.

"I *wish* we were late because of sex." I instantly regretted sharing something that felt like it was TMI for a first encounter.

We were all here for the same reasons, but the lack of sex worried me most. Aside from the plane fun, Evan and I hadn't fucked since our anniversary. A few weeks felt like forever, which was not a good thing because I really needed some dick, stat.

Wanting to avoid the awkward stares and exchanges like at the dog kennel, I opted to correct everyone and let them know that we weren't married but that we did live together and were pretty serious.

Vinh stood to do a quick headcount, ensuring all of his couples were accounted for and that their dietary needs had been met. This was definitely one of those times where I was glad to not have any restrictions because that pulled pork waiting for me smelled and looked bomb. Here's to hoping it tasted as good as it looks.

"Looks like everyone made it tonight." Vinh clapped, gaining everyone's attention. "As you all know, my name is Dr. Vinh Nguyen, and if you don't I'm a sex and intimacy therapist based in LA. I specialize in sex therapy, intimacy and I'm a kink educator specialist for those of you who don't identify as vanilla—yeah, I'm looking at you Carl and June," Vinh subtlety joked, dropping everyone's mouth, including my own.

My mind was like, '*Okay*' but my mouth was like '*What?*' Let me find out the oldest couple in the room a bunch of freaks.

Goals.

"One of the purposes of the icebreaker dinner, is to help ease some of the anxiety attached to group and individual therapy. In my experience for most couples, advising them during group sessions can be intimidating. Everyone feels like strangers. Everyone feels like their couple challenges feel individual. But people tend to open up more once we've learned a few things about one another. Plus, eating makes people way friendlier, and take it as a guy who attends munches. They're always a lot more fun when they're held at restaurants," he ended jovially.

"Now that I've gotten past that, here comes the hard part. I want everyone to introduce themselves but with a twist," he boldly stated, before letting everyone in on the twist.

Vinh wanted our partners to introduce us since he was under the impression that half of us would be too introverted to know what to say about ourselves. It sounded like a good idea in hindsight, but I hope no one hated each other here, because the thought of being here was awkward enough.

Having a look around, especially given that the ice-breaking task had started, there were all types of diverse couples at different stages in their lives. Black love couples, older couples, interracial couples, queer couples. There was even a polyamorous couple that had been quite entertaining trying to figure out who was going to introduce who.

When it was our turn, I tried to be subtle but descriptive. Focus on his background, his love for dogs, kids and basketball. Not to mention how annoyed he still got when people mentioned his height whenever meeting him for the first time.

Which, sadly, everyone *always* asked how tall he was.

I was good at talking up my man, but I regret going first in fear his response would be a read of me that I wasn't ready for. Imagine my surprise when he focused on the basics.

He started with the fact that I was a Black Dominican-American, something he joked that I would not be afraid to correct people on when they called me Spanish. I was surprised how perceptive he'd grown, detailing my experience from his own eyes and how I struggled between spaces that were bridges between identities for me. Evan gushed about me when he described the fact I had landed my dream job at a magazine, but I cringed when his statement led into a show asking a question about Vinh.

"She actually writes about sex and relationships. Kinda like you." He smiled but, since I knew him, I knew he was exercising his sarcastic tone.

"That's interesting," Vinh dismissed. "I'm pretty sure somewhere down the line, we have similar studies in common." I pinched Evan's thigh under the table, silently gesturing for him not to embarrass us.

"It kinda got me wondering, are you married at all? Or at least in a relationship?" *Look at him and his nosy ass.* Just *embarrassing.*

"That's actually a good question," Vinh countered, and while I took no pride in humbling my man, Vinh's answer had Evan feeling real cheap. Serves him right for being nosy.

"I was in a long-term relationship for a while. We didn't work for several reasons, but ones I'm comfortable sharing is that we communicated differently and we were never able to find a compromise that worked.

"We share a daughter together and used to co-parent but since I have full custody, my daughter has become my main priority until she's old enough to fully understand why her mother is not around like she used to be. Sometimes relationships aren't meant to be and not everyone you have a child with you're always meant to be with. It's a humbling, but a sad truth. But I let my experience drive my passion to help others."

With that, I shot Evan a look that screamed 'Boy, don't you ask this dude no more dumb questions', as once the dinner went on, accompanied by jokes, wine and great catering, Evan had finally eased up and became his usual gregarious self.

With a little wine in him, Evan struggled with not looking irritated every time Carl, the husband from the older couple kept calling him *big guy* instead of his own name, but he was taking it in stride by just pouring more wine.

I honestly couldn't wait for the dinner to end so everyone

could chat amongst themselves or better yet, who they gravitated toward most. Call me shocked when Evan gravitated toward the older couple, despite the husband not remembering his name, but I took that as they reminded him of his parents and he wanted to pick their brain about how long they've been in counseling, versus how long they had been married.

Their conversation took a tipsy turn when the wife bragged about how she was going to need a lot of bread and a decent hangover method if she were going to prepare for the yoga class in the morning, which if I didn't know any better, was the main reason she had come to the retreat in the first place.

"Once you're stretched out like that, you'll pretty much admit anything at that point," she joked, before I politely excused myself to mingle with some other sistas, or at least some of the queer folk.

With my luck, I didn't have to go far before someone introduced themselves to me. She was the only other Black woman who didn't have a Black partner and while no experience could ever be the same, since her partner was South Asian, it felt less lonely having someone who *kinda* knew what it felt like.

"Hi, I'm Renee," she said, holding her hand out for me to shake.

"Luz," I offered back, knowing we'd already introduce ourselves, but that it was polite to reintroduce ourselves talking one-on-one.

"This is your first time too?" She scrunched her nose, eyes searching the room, hugging her arms close to her body. She was about as nervous as I had been when I first thought about coming here, so I understood her reluctance.

"It is. My boyfriend and I are just getting over some communication problems, but we're hoping to get some tips on how to feel heard with certain topics. How about you?"

"Same, only with my husband. We've been married a few years so it's just been hard to get back to the honeymoon stage." I had to wonder what their issues were because they seemed so happy during the introduce-your-partner icebreaker. With my luck, I hadn't even had to ask, as after Evan's little twenty-one questions attempt, I wasn't trying to be in people's business.

"I think our biggest issue is that I've never actually met his family. The shitty thing about it is, he sees them. Spends time with them, shares some of his holidays with them. But either I'm not invited or they don't know that I exist. It's just frustrating. Do you have a similar experience?"

Remembering our first official milestone holiday as a couple, I'd totally bailed, making me realize how lucky I had been that within weeks of dating, he had wanted to introduce me to them. "No, but he comes from a super conservative family, so it could just have gone either way." I said, hoping that I didn't sound like I was being dismissive.

Evan never treated me like a dirty secret, but I certainly had a few of my own. I don't think I would have judged him if he had, because he was his own person and being with him is a whole lot easier when parents *aren't* involved.

In-laws were *not* fun. Point blank.

Spending most my night chatting up some of the other people of color, time flew fast because before I knew it, Evan and I were stripping down to our skivvies in our hotel room.

"C'mon," I murmured, kissing along his bare neck, hoping he would finally realize that this break from sex thing was whack. "I'm so horny," I whined.

"Luz, I'm, like, drunk as fuck. I probably couldn't stay hard if I wanted to," he retorted, before plopping on the left side of the bed.

Part of me was terrified Evan was losing his attraction for me. Another part was trying to be understanding that we had just gotten drunk. Word of advice. Never let a sixty-six year-old woman dare you to take four glasses of wine straight to the head. You ain't built like her.

Moaning a heavy sigh of frustration, I leaned in hoping Evan hadn't fallen asleep and gave him a good night kiss.

"Thank you, baby."

"For what?" he asked in a state of fatigue.

"For never being ashamed of me."

***

"Wakey, wakey. Mr. I-have-to-be-on-time-for-everything. This morning we have couples' yoga and I'm really not trying to miss that," I said as I changed into a new yoga set I've been dying to wear but just never got around to. Evan and his lazy behind was still in bed like it was a Sunday afternoon back home and not away on vacation.

"Luz. Come on. You said yesterday that all these things were optional. I'm not getting up at..." He looked over to his phone as his eyes widened in shock. "Six-thirty AM? That's too damn early for yoga. Wake me up when they're serving breakfast," he said, pulling the covers over his head like I was going to just let him lie there. Within seconds I was at the edge of the bed, taking a handful of the comforter into my hands and pulling it onto the floor to strip Evan of his sense of security.

"Boy, if you don't get up and come with me." He sat on his elbows, throwing his head back in frustration before he fixed his gaze back.

"You always jump at the chance to do this contortionist shit when you know I'm not as flexible as you." If I was more flexible than him, it was his fault. It was like his goal to test my limberness whenever he was in beast mode. The man would have me stretched out like Elastigirl if it meant he could get just *one* centimeter deeper.

"Evan, you'll be fine. You're in better shape than most people. Better shape than me. You think Betty White and Stan Lee out there are going to show you up," I joked as relief flooded through me when he decided to finally get his butt up and put some clothes on.

"I like the way your ass looks in those pants by the way," he said as we made our way to our couples' yoga class.

*****

As predicted, couples' yoga had been a bust. I, for one, was excellent at it, but Evan's jealousy only resulted in him disrupting the duration of the class by being a full-on trouble-maker. He did everything from tickle me to whisper things to throw me off my game. The last straw was when he dropped me in a couples' pose which made me eager to rush off to the scheduled breakfast because it was clear he was in a famished mood.

The next activity after a much-needed breakfast involved another group session where we were paired off into doubles. Lucky for Evan, our partners were the only other couple that didn't annoy him, so he was much more pleasant in the exercise portion that felt more like a game of Family Feud than it did in a bonding exercise. Evan wasn't the best at faking having fun so I took his genuine engagement and smiling as a sign that he was having a decent time.

"Okay, five seconds to get your answers down. Things you should hate that your partner does but secretly love. Time and *go*," our partner couple announced as we rushed to scribble our answers down on our personal dry erase boards. That one was easy for me because I knew Evan wouldn't get it, considering it contradicted my need to want to look polished all the time. But if I could take a guess his would probably say something like, when you yell the TV screen. He claimed he hated it but I knew he found it hilarious.

"All right times up. Evan, what was your guess?" With furrowed brows, he thought long and hard before he answered and disciplined me with just a look when I turned to reveal that he was wrong.

"When I play in your hair? *Come on.* You always tell me to stop when I do."

"Okay, yeah, but I don't always to *mean* it," I admitted smugly. He practically lived to contribute to my frizz and separate my curls but I don't know, there was something so calming about someone playing in your hair. I still wasn't going to stop scolding him for doing it though.

"All right. You're never gonna guess mine then. We're basically down seven to zero." Our couple friends were definitely killing it in the knowing everything about each other department, something I wasn't trying to make myself feel bad for because who *wanted* to know every damn thing about each other? Some things were just better off a mystery.

"What is your partner's favorite memory of you together? This time we'll do ten seconds. Ready?" With so many memories to choose from, I couldn't think of one time that would stand out to him. Seeing the world through different lenses we definitely had different interpretations on what we considered great moments. There was this one time we watched movies in Central Park and last Christmas we did the whole exchanging gifts things at his parents' house. He got a ton of his relatives to surprise me with cheesy things I grew up wanting that my mom didn't always have the money for after my dad died. It was obvious he had gotten some old wish lists from my mom because half of the stuff I didn't even remember until it was staring me in the face. I took a deep breath finally jotting down my answer, knowing for sure he wouldn't even remember this weekend getaway. For some reason I felt compelled to remind him of something that solidified me wanting to spend my life with him. I wonder what he wrote down?

"Time's up." Since we were on our last question before a

break, we volunteered to just turn them over at the same time. My mouth fucking dropped seeing his answer match mine.

"*Vermont*? Damn, I can't believe we finally got one." He laughed as our partners really tried insulting us by tallying up the scores like we didn't get every one of them wrong.

"Okay, everyone, we're going to take a brief intermission before we start the next group session. Today, I have with me an amazing colleague who's going to be conducting sessions since I have a few requests for some private counseling. Her name is Dr. Alice Charbonnier, and it's a pleasure to have her here. We've worked together countless times, and if you're going to have someone assess and discover solutions for your current dilemmas, there is no better person I trust than her."

"Mon cheri, you flatter me. But do keep going, an old lady like me never gets tired of hearing compliments." She smiled warmly. While she was older, it didn't take away from the fact that she was freaking gorgeous. Her silver white hair almost made it look intentional. I mean homegirl could probably still bag a partner in their twenties through forties easy with her youthful personality. When I reached her age, I hoped my body still looked like that. Her accent sounded somewhat French, but I wasn't an expert on region or country. If I had to take my guess I'd say she was from Europe though.

"Hey, I'm gonna go to the bathroom really quick," Evan said, and I volunteered to go with him because I just needed a quick break away from the crowd. Choosing the closest bathroom, Evan and I waited a bit before deciding to hit the one up closer to the lodging because with how long it was taking them, it was bound to be unbearable to breathe in there. Walking gave me a chance to probe him about our last answer.

"Sooooo...Vermont, huh? I know why I said Vermont, but I'm curious to why you did. It was pretty much an uneventful trip. We didn't even have any type of nasty sex or anything. It rained. We slept. We ate. Nothing really special about it," I admitted. And I was right. There wasn't really anything extraordinary about that trip and only meant something special to me. On my father's death anniversary, I always got really down and just needed to get away. I don't know how long I've been doing it for but it was long before Evan and sometimes I just needed to be somewhere that helped me take my mind off all the things that burdened me. Even on the short notice Evan understood that. Evan always understood.

"Hmph...you probably don't remember it the way I do. That first night you could barely get to sleep, and that was even after tea and meditating and all that other stuff you like to do to clear your mind. When you finally did fall asleep you tossed and turned all night. I remember flipping over because I wasn't getting any sleep anyway, so I took a chance and put my arms around you. You were just so quiet after that. And still. I had never seen you more peaceful. That's when I knew that was what I wanted. A peaceful life with you. That's why I chose Vermont."

All these couples with their serious problems had me feeling remorse that me and Evan's worst problem was that I didn't want to get married. People here were struggling with infidelity, being hidden from their partner's families, and here I was just dragging us out here to throw in people's faces that other than this *one* issue, we had a solid relationship. They were going to hate us after this next group session. When we finally made it to the bathroom, Evan leaned in to give me a kiss on the forehead.

"I'll be out in a minute, but just so you know one of those private session requests came from me." Figured as much. I guess we wouldn't be sharing our woes with the group after all.

CHAPTER ELEVEN

Luz

"So, how's everyone doing? Having fun yet?" Vinh smiled as he sat down on an identical bean bag chair to ours to meet us on the floor. Fun wasn't the first thing to come to mind, but we were definitely in a calmer place than we first arrived.

It was easy to forget you had problems like bills and relationship issues, when you were surrounded by a peaceful environment, free of police sirens and car horns. "Yeah, we're having something," Evan said with a sarcastic rant to his voice.

Now that we were in private, it was easier to discuss our specific issues, as I knew Evan wouldn't divulge too much to our retreat buddies. "So, part of my process with the one-on-ones is trying to uncover the root of your problems, so I can help you come up with solutions to help you overcome them on your own. Some couples don't know how to define what's not working, whereas others are dealing with a few specific issues and feel overwhelmed trying to focus on the most tangible one, hoping the rest just resolves themselves on their own.

The number one issue I come across is lack of communication. Partners aren't communicating, holding a lot in and therefore, making it worse." He laughed a jovial guffaw.

"Nothing ever resolves itself on its own, but some couples just lack effective communication skills because they haven't been taught them. Do you think either of you have that problem?"

In unison, we turned to look at each other. Evan could have easily gone first, but when the question was sparked, I figured we would have separate opportunities to voice our thoughts. "Do you want to tackle this or do you want me to?" He shrugged.

"Maybe I can go first and if you disagree, you can jump in." He nodded in agreement, allowing me to fix my gaze back on our counselor.

"Honestly, Evan and I don't have an issue communicating. He tells me what's on his mind *most* of the time. We don't always agree on things, but we always seem to come to an understanding. From my point of view, the only major arguments we've had have been the few weeks leading up to us deciding to come here. Other than that, it's been like, petty arguments." I ended with a dragged out *yeah* not knowing of more to add.

Gesturing toward Evan, Vinh and I both shifted our attention toward him. "Do you have anything to add to that, Evan?" His question forcing me to chew on my lips out of nervousness, but relieved to learn we were at least on the same page with how we viewed our relationship.

"No, she's right. Communication isn't our specific issue. Luz is actually incredible at making sure I know when I'm not being the partner she needs. I'd say I'm about the same. When we first got together, she was a little unyielding, but over the past few months she's been amazing at considering my needs and feelings, especially in regards to our relationship."

I let out a huge sigh that I'd been holding on to, relieved that he actually recognized my efforts. Vinh brought his hands together in a clap and with every second that passed, I tried focusing on a trait of his obsessed fan base probably went nuts over to divert away from my nerves.

First it was his muscular arms. Then it was his untamed cowlick. Dude had a whole checklist more but I tried focusing on the things that wouldn't show how anxious I was. "Actually, that's great. Lots of people don't know how to effectively communicate with their partners, so you're definitely a step ahead of the rest. So, the second thing I see most common in couples, is intimacy, or rather *lack* of intimacy.

Straightening up, Evan raised his hand with the quickness of a teacher's pet, eager to share his knowledge and expertise. "Can I take this one, baby?"

My eyes widened, despite nodding my confirmation, as I was positive he wouldn't have let me answer if I wanted to. "I don't want to come off as a braggart but if we have to spend ten minutes talking about our sex life, it's gonna sound like we don't have any problems, because our sex life is amazing. Luz is the first person I've been with to take me out of my comfort zone. Hell, half the time I can't even keep up with her. But someone's got to take the job, so it might as well be me." My hand met his shoulder in a hard slap.

"Clown ass." All he could do was shrug with a dopey smile on his face like the king of all jesters.

"What? Come on, I was complimenting you. Did you want me to lie?" I didn't want him to fabricate it, but I certainly felt some kind of way that he hadn't mentioned the fact that we hadn't been sexually active as of late, which for the record wasn't like us.

"You don't have to make it sound like a chore," was my only retort as Evan tilted my chin to meet his intense gaze.

"Look at me. Being intimate with you is never a chore." There was a genuine sincerity in his tone so when he leaned in for a soft, simple kiss, all it did was leave me starving for more.

"I can go down the list of common relationship issues but having a chance to observe you privately, it's evident that the both of you are in a very different place than the other couples that I meet with. You're openly affectionate. You respect one another and you don't talk over each other. You don't know how rare that is. Interrupting and talking over one another is usually a clear sign people don't feel seen or heard. So, my question is what sparked the decision for both of you to come here. To add on to that, what would you like to accomplish before you leave?"

Gulp! This was one question that would bring us back to Earth. Evan gave me a look as I silently gave my approval that he was better equipped to answer this question. "Luz and I don't agree on big life changes. I want to get married but she doesn't want to. We've been living together for close to a year now, but the topic of marriage didn't come up until I planned to propose.

"I wasn't under the impression that she felt so strongly about the subject, especially since until now, we've never discussed it. The topic of having kids and moving out of the city to buy a house was something we both wanted, but I just don't see how any of that can happen if she doesn't see herself getting married. Those are all the things I planned on reserving for my future wife, not just a girl I'm dating."

Wow. So now I was just a girl he was dating. Not the woman who comforted him. Not the woman who nursed him back to health when he was sick. Not the woman who organized Super Bowl parties for him and all his little sports-obsessed friends. Just the girl he was dating. I'd hate to see how he referred to a fuck buddy. Now that he stopped talking, it was time for me to defend myself.

"The way I see it, I want kids. I want to get out of the city into someplace more residential. I just don't see why we need a piece of paper to do it. A piece of paper won't change the way I feel about him. Loads of people get married and just legit change on each other. I just want us to stay the same. The way we were before all this engagement drama. What we have is everything

I've ever dreamed of in a healthy relationship. I don't want any of that to change."

Vinh looked to both of us, pinching his chin with detailed concern. "Do you know what it is you love about each other?"

My eyes squinted in confusion, Evan's expression matching mine, when I took the time to study his reaction. Maybe we both knew but just didn't tell each other?

"Okay, let's try something. Forget all your problems for a solid five minutes. I want you to tell each other what you love about them and what you love about your relationship. Only caveat is, I want you to face each other. Look into each other's eyes, *without* looking down or away. I find that emotions are felt more intensely when you're looking directly into someone's eyes when you reveal personal things."

The instructions sounded easy enough. Together, we both adjusted ourselves on our beanbag chairs so we were face-to-face, but it felt more like a staring contest than a heart-to-heart because neither one of us could take this shit seriously without making funny faces at each other, which resulted in obnoxious, echoing laughter.

"Come on, Luz, stop being a goofball. We're wasting this man's time. On three. One. Two. Three," he counted down but I couldn't help myself. I made the ugliest face I can muster just to send this man crying.

"Luz, I fucking hate you," he replied while giving into the same instinct to do the same thing he was shaming me for.

"I feel like I should go first because I have a feeling he'll try to sabotage me by trying to make me laugh after he admitted all his reasons." Evan's brow furrowed in annoyance as he curled his lip.

"Go ahead, Luz, I'm not stopping you." Not even a second later, Evan crossed his eyes in a way that creeped me out at first but always brought me to tears. Evan could cross one eye while the other stayed in the center and he knew that shit tripped me out.

"Oh my god. Can you tell him to take this seriously?" I whined to our counselor, but all he had for me was a huge joyful smile on his face.

"You two are a blast. I love to see it."

Evan slapped my thigh to grab my attention, promising that he would behave if I could do the same. I took a deep breath opening my eyes and straightening up to center on his. Evan had such beautiful eyes. I can't believe I got to stare into these babies every day.

"So, let me start with the obvious. One of the things I love most about you are your eyes but not for the reason you think." His brows furrowed in confusion but was doing as he was told by not looking down or away from me. It was beginning to feel intimidating. "Sure, your eyes are a pretty shade of green, but that isn't what I like about them. It's the way you look at things when you're focused or confused. Even when you bless me with a cocky smile. Your eyes are so wild and expressive. When you look at me there's this sense of knowing, this sense of belonging and feeling like I fit somewhere. Even if it's just in your eyes." Tucking my lips in, I had to remind myself not to look down. This shit was harder than it looked.

"I love how you make me laugh. Even when I'm mad at you. Your bravery of looking ridiculous is unmatched. And I found out the hard way that I love that." A wide smile lit up his face as I recalled the last time I spent with him and his kids while they were trying to teach this old geezer how to do TikTok dances. It was hilarious. "I love that you hold me accountable when I mistreat you. I try my best to shower you with the acts you love most and I'll admit, I'm trying and you're being so patient. I love that you took a chance on me because I know I'm not always the easiest to love. I don't say it enough but that means so much to me." Looking into his eyes did make it more intense. I hadn't realized how hard it was to focus on someone, even someone you saw every day and reveal vulnerable truths. I wiped a lone tear that escaped my eye and exhaled a deep breath I hadn't realize I was holding.

"Wow, that was intense. It's hard doing that when you can't look down or away." Now it was Evan's turn, only with him he interlocked his long fingers in mine making it all the more intimate.

"You know one of the things I love about you is that I know your love doesn't come easy. You don't just give it away. You make people earn it. Ever since the day I met you, it's been your beliefs, your passion, and your caution that have encouraged me into becoming a man that somehow deserves you. The way you view the world helps me reassess my blind spots and how I can be an overall better person. Because I know how hard it can be when challenging people you love. I love that you believe in second chances. If you hadn't we wouldn't be here today. When I saw you at that bar at that speed dating event, I just kept thinking, man, this is one of the wildest examples of kismet if I ever saw one. When I tell our story to others, it always felt like that. A story. A story that I never want to end. I love that you trust me with your body, your pleasure and your heart. You say you're hard to love but for me loving you is like breathing, it's instinctual. The way you let me to take care of you in the ways that I'm good at, without forcing me in ways that I'm not. I love that I can tell you these things. Things some might accuse a man of being beta or less masculine for. With you I'm my most vunerable. There isn't a side to me that you don't see."

If there was one thing Evan knew how to do outdo me on, it was anything and everything that involved this relationship. It was one thing to know someone loved you, another to express it so eloquently. I didn't always look at us as perfect, but in rare moments like this, maybe we were.

"While you still have her close to you, why don't you tell Luz why marriage is so important to you?" For the first time since the exercise, Evan looked down, stroking my hands before he fixed his gaze back toward me.

"For me, marriage is a lifelong commitment. A promise that we'll be there for each other. The final seal on how we already feel for one another. Finding out you don't want to get married is a huge deal breaker for me, because while you don't see yourself getting married, I do. I don't see how we can last feeling so differently about it. If there was one thing that could force us apart, it would be this." He answered truthfully, and just like that my heart shattered into a million pieces.

I both validated and respected his thoughts on the subject but didn't understand how someone who just gave all these beautiful reasons on why he loved me could switch his position over the topic of marriage. While we both shared a Catholic background, we weren't even practicing, so religion wasn't even a good enough excuse. If he only knew the real reason I didn't want to get married, maybe just *maybe* he'd give me room to breathe. But what if it didn't change anything? What if by telling him, things only got worse? It had been my burden to bear for so long, reliving the past was like reliving that trauma and I never wanted to find myself in a situation like that again.

"Luz, why don't you confide in Evan why marriage scares you?" Vinh asked, snapping me out of my trance. Feeling defeated, I broke away from Evan's hands.

"Because I don't want us to change. People change when they exchange vows, and I just want us to stay the way we are. What's wrong with how we are?" I asked, playing with my hands, my eyes casting downward. With the crook of his fingers, Evan lifted my chin to meet his eyes. There was a sadness there I hated seeing, but I had to be honest about my feelings otherwise I'd lose him.

"Luz, why would we change? You'll still be you and I'll still be me," he said as knots coiled in my stomach, knowing that wasn't something he could guarantee.

"Evan, you don't know that. That's not something you can

promise me." He looked down and away from me, twirling the simple band on his index finger.

"Then we're doomed before we even begin." It hurt knowing he saw no future for us. I turned back to our counselor unsure of where to go from here, a sense of relief washing over me when he chose to end the awkward silence.

"It's too early to declare any relationship over until you've both given up, and from how Luz feels, it's clear that she's not giving up. When was the last time you worked together on something? Not housework or planning a trip, but something that helps you address your strengths and weaknesses?" I pondered silently, trying to recall us working together on *anything*. We lived in the city and anytime something broke or we got some new furniture, Evan would just pull out his credit cards and pay someone to fix it, just to grant us some kind of peace. We never gave ourselves opportunities to work together outside of budgeting, planning and adult shit no one was excited to do. Reaching in back of him, Vinh pulled out a fishbowl filled with folded up pieces of paper and slid it over to us, landing near Evan's bare feet.

"In there are a bunch of activities that will force you to work together. That's if you don't kill each other first." Evan picked up the fishbowl, placing it in his lap awaiting instructions.

"This is one of my more *successful* exercises. Most couples reach a breakthrough by the next day." Instead of arguing on who would decide the exercise we'd participate in, we rock-paper-scissored it, earning Evan the right to choose. He swirled his hand in the bowl, pulling out a folded piece of paper as he read the note aloud.

"Together we will build a campsite. All supplies will be included but will exclude proper instructions. In order to be successful, you will have to work as a team to set up your beautiful campsite. This is right up my alley," he bragged. It was just like Evan to pick one of the many things *he* was good at.

CHAPTER TWELVE

Evan

"I know you're happy," Luz chastised as she lazily sipped on her water bottle, while I was stuck taking time to unload the materials for the tent. We were supposed to be figuring it out together. It took us less than an hour away from the retreat to find a decent campsite but half of that hour was spent having to hear Luz complain about my chosen exercise. "The one thing we have to do to work together and you pick something I'm shit at just so you can spend the day bossing me around." I turned around from my organizing to find her digging through the bag of tools. If she did more *helping* and less *talking*, maybe we would have been done already.

"Luz, no one can boss *you* around. Certainly not me. While you're looking through that bag, mind handing me the mallet?"

"The what?" she asked with a straight face. I know she didn't make a habit of going around fixing things but, as smart as Luz was, putting things together was *not* her specialty. I had the book-cases and coffee tables to prove it.

"Babe, could you just hand me that one that looks like a hammer. I don't know how you've gone your whole life without ever going camping." Laying down the footprint, I decided to add the tarp down just in case. With the predicted forecast of rain tonight, I wasn't taking any chances. Luz rolled her eyes when she passed me the mallet. "Ugh! Sometimes I think you forget you're dating a Black girl who grew up poor and in the hood. The only campsite I was building was in my imagination." She scoffed. *Duh*, I used to drive her home every day, but even the kids I coached had gone camping on school trips. She couldn't use that excuse forever.

"Well, when we have kids, I'm going to make it a habit of regularly taking them camping. That's if we even make it that far." Luz threw down one of the tents pieces stomping away to leave me to figure all this out on my own. Fortunately, I was knowledge-able enough when it came to installing since my dad and I did this all the time. I could put the damn thing together by myself, but it would be a whole lot faster if she wasn't using every excuse in the world to walk away.

"Gosh, Evan. Why do you have to say shit like that?"

"I'm just thinking out loud. Would you rather me keep it to myself because *you're* the one who dragged me half across the country to come here? We could have been in Italy right now, or fucking Jamaica," I snapped. Months prior to my botched proposal, we were in talks to go somewhere tropical or someplace historic, but this was how we were spending our winter vacation together. She didn't get to tell me to keep my feelings to myself when the whole reason we were here was to fix our relationship. Like a petulant child, she marched back just to get the final word.

"I just hate it when you're in a shitty mood. You just get grumpy and sarcastic. I don't see why you can't just take my word that I'm committed to you. Why is marrying you the only way to prove it?" By now, I was sick of explaining myself. I just wanted to build this damn tent before it started to rain and get dark, but of course my Italian blood made it impossible for me to stand down an argument. Just once I wish I could just let shit go.

"Because it's important to me, Luz. All the things I do that are important to you, I don't question it. You know I'm traditional, you knew that about me when we first met. You knew that when we got back together. You knew that when you moved in with me. What? Did you think I was never going to ask you?" Truthfully, I knew Luz was a little less traditional with her thoughts on relationships, I just didn't think that she was so new age that she would discount marriage.

"Urgh! I don't know. But if you think me not wanting to get married is the thing that dooms us, I don't know how to change your mind. Telling you isn't good enough and showing you isn't good enough, either." Maybe she was right. I was so clouded by my own anger I never stopped to think about all the ways she had changed for me. Things that I hadn't asked her to do, just things she picked up along the way. Laying out my clothes in the morning. Making me coffee. Surprising me with my favorite dishes after she knew I had a long day at work. Luz wasn't naturally nurturing, but she did those things because she knew my love language. While she wasn't comfortable with me paying all the bills at first, she recognized that was the way I took care of her. In an Italian home, men took care of their families. They took care of their wives. Being financially independent, I knew that was the hardest thing for Luz to overcome. But she did. All just to be with me.

When Luz began gathering up the pieces of the alternate, much smaller tent included in the given supplies, it was clear she was doing her own thing by trying to build the less complicated one by herself. She set herself up several feet away from mine, giving me the silent treatment but after measuring her frustration, I ended the silence.

"Do you even know what you're doing?" She threw a piece back into her organized mess of a pile and stood.

"No, but if you're going to be grumpy all night, I'd rather just sleep by myself. You're not the only one who can demand alone time," she added with a childish stuck out tongue. I could totally let her figure it out on her own without warning her, but the rain was supposed to be bad tonight and if she didn't set it up properly, there would be no barrier between her and the rainstorm. I wasn't *that* upset with her.

"You're probably not going to listen to me, but that's probably not the best idea. You might break something because you've never done this before. Plus, the weather is supposed to be terrible. The bigger tent is built to withstand that kind of thing. If you fumble, even with one piece, that thing is *not* going to protect you." She let out a cry of frustration.

"Evan. I don't care. I'll take my chances with the storm. Because it's obvious we both need time to cool off." Going back to my own project, I got in a quick 'fine, suit yourself" and was almost shocked that she didn't challenge me for the last word.

***

The sounds of a storm never failed to soothe me. The uncomfortable silence between Luz and I had given me anxiety, and it took me forever to fall asleep. The second the sound of rain pattered against the canvas, it was the lullaby I knew I needed. Usually I was a hard sleeper, I had to be living with Luz, Mary, and our new dog, Carmelo. However, the sound of someone whimpering and tapping at the tents entrance coaxed me out of the few hours I actually did manage to get.

Crawling out of my sleeping bag, I switched the lanterns on switch and staggered over to unzip the tent door open. There stood a soaking wet Luz, her clothes and hair drenched from the inevitable rain. Rather than chastise her, I pulled her inside, her body shivering so violently that her teeth were actually chattering. "Hold on, let me get you a towel and dry clothes." I rushed toward my bag and pulled out a long beach towel and black crewneck. All my other sweat pants were back at the retreat site, but since I had boxers on underneath, I offered her mine. With a spare t-shirt, I helped her soak some of the water that weighed down her soaking wet hair.

"I was fine until the rain caused my tent to collapse," she said in between sniffles. It was almost adorable. "So I skipped a few crucial steps. I didn't know I'd wake up to a wall of water." Trying hard to bite my tongue, I fought the urge to say I told you since it was clear she had learned her lesson. What good would it do to rub it in?

"Not sure you what you want me to say." One leg at a time, she slipped out of her pants and tank top to change into the clothes I gave her. Her braless tits looked more tempting than I should have allowed myself to notice, as her nipples hardened from being out in the cold.

"If you need to hear me say it, fine." She took a deep breath and faked a smile. "You're better at this sort of thing than me, and I should have just listened to you." Remember when I said I wouldn't rub it in? Well, now the circumstances had changed.

"I'm sorry, what?" I approached her, cupping my hand over my ear to get her to repeat it. Her smile wavered into pressed lips that barely wanted to get the words out.

"I said I should have listened to you. You were right." With suppressed enthusiasm, I punched the air.

"Luz, the sweetest sound to leave your mouth is when you admit to me when you're wrong. Wooo, boy. It doesn't happen often but when it does, it tops the lyrics to my favorite song. Now get your stubborn ass over here so you can warm up." She dropped the towel to the floor with her pile of wet clothes, making herself comfortable in my embrace. We stood there silent for a brief moment as she buried her head in my chest like a lost little puppy, still sniffling and anxious to get warm.

"Let's lay down," I suggested after kissing her forehead and leading her to my oversized sleeping bag. She curled up against me laying her head on my chest, as my fingers played in her wet curls. Her hair hung longer when it was wet, nearly down to her shoulders. When dry, it sat up high in a curly fro. As much as I loved her hair in its dry, coily roundness, there was this delicateness to her when she wore it like this. Especially now since she was free of her usual face of makeup. "You stubborn woman." I pressed another kiss to her forehead, resulting in her turning up to look at me.

"Feel better?" Her face cinched.

"Yeah, a little." She purred, while pulling her legs up and making a home for her icy cold feet in between my unexpected thighs. I flinched at the drop the in temperature, but figured for what she endured, she deserved some kind of relief.

"Would you warn me before you do that? My balls are practically the size of walnuts right now. It's like I took a cold shower."

"Sorry," she apologized as she lifted up to rest her chin on my chest, gazing up at me with curious feline eyes.

"You're so quiet. What are you thinking about" Hell, what wasn't I thinking about? Her. Me. Us. Where the both of us would be a year from now. It's weird how you could be so sure about something, so sure about *someone* and then not have any control over whether your relationship started or ended. We couldn't go back home without coming to some kind of conclusion. As a man, I had time to waste. Which most men did in effort to become the man they wanted to be. There was no time clock ticking for when I could become a father and no double standard if I decided to walk away from Luz and just be with a younger woman with a less complicated way of looking at marriage and relationships. To most, I would have been well within my right to choose that path. Unfortunately, when it came to loving her, I was just as stubborn as she was admitting she was wrong. I only wanted her as my wife. Why didn't she want me as her husband?

"I don't know, baby. This trip is just really getting to me. I'm not sure I'm having fun," I admitted as she mounted me while I propped my head up with one arm and rested the other cupping her curvy ass.

"Evan, do you know how much I love you?" I exhaled a deep, frustrated sigh. Of course, I did. She would have never persuaded me to come here if I hadn't. The old Luz avoided her problems, but the one I had been dating for over a year faced her challenges head on. That was one thing that had changed drastically about her since we first started dating. I had to give her credit.

"Yes, Luz, I do." She ran her fingers through my hair, later finding herself tracing my full eyebrows.

"And how do you know that?" Another deep sigh.

"From the way you take care of me. And the way you've sacrificed for me. I know we wouldn't be here if you didn't love me."

"So then you know how much I'm invested in our relationship. Evan, I sold my condo. That was pretty much the only valuable thing I've ever owned. But I did so to be closer to you. Because I like waking up next to you. I like coming home to you. My best friend and coworkers have had enough me bragging about you, but I don't care because that's how proud I am to call you my man. But these past few weeks, I feel like you've been punishing me." I grimaced, unsure of what she meant.

"Baby, how am I punishing you?" Raising her hand to her temple, she shook her head and straightened out her hand just centimeters away from my face.

"Well, for starters, we're not really having sex."

"Luz, you're being dramatic. We had sex a few days ago." She silenced me with a finger to my lips.

"No. You used a toy on me to help me with my anxiety. It's like this whole marriage thing has you all grouchy, and when you're grouchy, it's like you barely want to touch me." Squeezing her ass, I leaned up to give her a light kiss on the mouth.

"Nonsense. I always want to touch you." I leaned up to kiss her a second time, only this time was longer with a lot more tongue. "I'm sorry if I made you feel that way. I think I'm just dealing with a lot because we always mostly agree on things. Maybe it's affected my sex drive a little. But I promise it's not forever, okay? Can I have a kiss?"

This time she met me for one, a light laugh escaping her mouth when I gave her ass another squeeze. Imagine my surprise when she rolled off me and wished me a good night before turning her back to me to go to sleep. I put my arm around her, the aromatic scent of Moroccan oil lingering in her damp hair. Pushing the thick curly tendrils to the side, I nestled the length of her throat graduating to light kisses at the back of her neck. With a firm grip on her right breast she moaned in frustration as she lightly pushed me away.

"Evan, stop if you're just gonna tease me." Pulling her firm, round ass away from my crotch only forced me to scoot closer to her, but this time I held her tighter so she couldn't run away. Nibbling on her ears, she shivered at the sensation, reminding me that she was so ticklish there.

"Why would I tease you?" She finally gave in, pressing her lower body into mine, my erection growing at the promise of being inside her. "One of these days you have to tell me your secret. How you can make me hard as a rock in a pair of my sweat pants and baggy ass t-shirt." As much as I loved her in lingerie, I'd found her equally sexy in something that disguised her curves. Maybe it was her scent, her confidence, her sensuality, or the fact that Luz could pull off anything. Either way, I missed her like crazy and by the way she whimpered as I ravished her shoulders in kisses, the feeling was mutual. Her back was extremely sensitive and for that reason, it was my favorite spot to kiss her. Sometimes it was too much sensation for her to handle but with our brief break, she seemed to endure it like a pro.

"Take off your clothes for me," I whispered, helping her out of her borrowed pants and top, revealing her amazing body. The woman had everything I went nuts over, from her full breasts, round ass, and sexy legs that went on for miles. Legs that if I set out the time and had no other plans, I could spend hours between coaxing her to sheer madness. Finding my hand between her legs, I bit my lip at the sign of her soaking wetness. "You're already so wet, baby. Did you miss me that much?" I whispered, swirling my fingers against her swollen nub and wet folds. I knew what I wanted, but knew this was what she needed from all the days that I denied her intimacy. All she wanted was for me to be inside her and had every intention on fulfilling her wish.

Luz propped up on her knees and elbows, giving me direct access to her ass and pussy from behind. Lowering my mouth to taste her, she squirmed at the way my greedy tongue lapped against her clit and pussy lips, licking and sucking her like it was my last meal. The sounds she made fed my hunger. The desperate way she rode my face told me just how bad she needed this. Needed me. But as much as I wanted her to come on my face, the ache in my cock just had to feel her.

"Mmmm...tell me you want me to fuck you." My mouth breathy and hot between licking her clean.

"Oh fuck, Evan. I want you to fuck me," she replied, wanting, breathless and eager for more. Slapping her ass, I leaned up and took my shirt and boxers off, positioning her hips right where I needed her. The sight of her ass was enough to make anyone tempted to slap it but if I had it my way, this ass was mine and would always be mine. If only she knew what she did to me. Without warning, I pushed my heavy erection against her tight wet opening, as we groaned and gasped in unison at the initial first thrust. The way her muscles gripped me had me tempted to take things slow, but the fire coursing from my body to hers brought forth another course of action. Before I knew it, slow strokes became fast strokes and shallow thrusts became deep ones. Her breath came in jagged gasps now, moans dying in her mouth before they could become words. I pistoned harder, in and out until my cock was covered in her beautiful juices, sweat lining my skin as I bent down to reach my hand between her legs to work her clit while I fucked her. She let out a cry so beautiful it nearly took me off my game, but my body was on a mission. Its only purpose now was to make her come.

"You like that, baby? You like it when I play with your pussy while I fuck you?" Her heavy gasping and strained face told me everything I needed to know but there was nothing like hearing the words. "Come on, baby. Talk to me. Don't you love this fat cock in your pussy?" At that she arched her back lower, allowing me in deeper as she matched me thrust for thrust.

"Oh fuck, papi. You're gonna make me come." Leaning back up, I gripped her hips, the sound of sweat slicked skin slapping filling the tent. "What's wrong, baby? I know you want to come." Her cries heightened with every time our bodies touched, only now I was matching her rhythm as she ground her reckless hips into mine.

"Just like that, Papi. I'm so fucking close." At her command, I rocked into her just like she liked it, anxious to release my selfish load, but determined for her to give in first. As if on cue her body spasmed updating me on her current state. Thank god she was on her way. When my pace quickened, her cries came out more like screams and at this point I didn't need any more concentration, I was ready to give in.

"Oh fuck, I'm about to come." She repeated until her words were barely audible and in three shuttering thrusts, I pounded hard, letting out a rough groan as I blew into her with the force of a storm. Coming inside her was the icing on the cake after a primal fuck, and nothing had me feeling closer to her when we decided to stop using condoms. Still inside her, I bent down to kiss her neck, out of breath and dripping in sweat.

"Damn it, I fucking love you. You know that?" She turned around as the taste of salt was still heavy on her lips when she reached into kiss me.

"Maybe I should accuse you of not wanting me every day.

Especially if you fuck me like that." Wrapping my arms around her, we leaned up as I nibbled on her ear.

"Baby, I always want you. Please stop saying that." I pressed a soft kiss to her cheek. "Want a towel?" She nodded, my body feeling cold when I broke away from our heat. I pulled out the only other towel I had to help her dry off for a second time that night.

"All good?"

"Yep," she confirmed as we crawled back into the sleeping bag, feeling suddenly cold until she got comfortable in my arms.

"Evan, I love you," she said, interlocking her slender brown fingers in mine as I leaned in to kiss her cheek.

"I love you too, baby. Now get some sleep," I said prematurely, the sound of her light snoring letting me know she was already there.

***

I woke up to a spacious sleeping bag, my eyes blinking in and out several times before they fully opened. As my blurred vision cleared, Luz was up bright and early, putting her clothes back on and folding whatever she had on the night before in one neat pile. I yawned, rolling back in my sleeping spot.

"Damn. You're up early. Going somewhere?" She walked over to me, sitting down cross legged. Lazily, I reached my hand to her upper thigh.

"Come back and lay with me." She took a deep sigh, pulling my arm until I sat straight up, creases of worry etched on her sweet face.

"Evan, there's something I wanted to talk to you about." Grabbing my boxers , I judged her by her expression that it was serious because she only looked at me that way when something bad had happened. I had a feeling I should be partially dressed for it.

"I've been struggling with a way to tell you this. I wasn't even sure I was going to, but I feel like you deserve to know the real reason I don't want to get married." I stood straight up.

"Okay?" Drawing it out, she took another deep sigh. Just fucking spit it out.

"Evan. The real reason I don't want to get married is because....it's because I've already been married before." And like that, her truth hit me like a punch to the gut.

CHAPTER THIRTEEN

Luz

I'd bore witness to a multitude of Evan's common expressions and could almost always predict how the conversation would go according to said expressions. Furrowed brows wide-eyed expression was his confused look. Something that was usually followed with a dozen questions regarding something he didn't understand, like how the battle systems of the video games I liked required leveling up in a way he had found to be boring.

There was also his "I want to fuck you" look, where with a cock of his eyebrow and a sinister grin, I knew to expect something fun happening in the next few minutes. That expression I got almost seventy-five percent of the time and I was never disappointed by what followed. The one I dreaded most was when he was angry with me. I didn't see it a lot and truthfully, I wasn't seeing it now. The look on his face was one I almost didn't recognize since it wasn't often. His usual bright green eyes dimmed to a sickly, sallow khaki. Until now, I didn't even know his eyes could look that way and I hated being the reason for it. I guess there was a first time for everything.

"What?" He lowered his gaze, suddenly realizing he wasn't fully dressed as he gathered his shirt and slipped into some pants.

"I said....that the reason I don't want to get married isn't because I don't want to. It's because I did a stupid thing way before we reconnected. Evan, it was the biggest mistake I've *ever* made in my life. I can't go through that again." When you grow up in a conservative home, no one ever prepares you about dating or intense feelings or how to spot signs of toxic love. My last *real* relationship before Evan was the latter. Like past relationships, things started out intense, from zero to one hundred in what felt like months. Before I knew it, I became someone's wife and that's when all the problems started. "Who..." He hesitated, his gaze lowering. "Who were they?" He asked, centering his gaze back on me, his green eyes dimming to a pit of darkness and detachment, like he wasn't entirely there.

"Umm...does it matter who he was?"

"It matters to me."

Taking a huge sigh, I started from the beginning. His name was Antonio Velasquez and I met him just as I'd graduated from college. At the time I was on a no-guys-strike, mainly because after my high school breakup with Evan, I wasn't sure I even wanted another guy in my head. High school love had hardened me, but it didn't stop me from falling for Antonio.

Antonio was everything I was positive I didn't want. Cocky, possessive but so irresistibly charming. Not to mention relentless. He wormed his way into my heart and with things I was going through at the time, I let myself be vulnerable. The same way I'd let Evan in seventeen years ago. So, on my twenty-fourth birthday, when he asked me to marry him, I felt like the luckiest girl in the world. Meanwhile, our relationship was changing. The past encouragement and compliments turned into resentment and jealousy. My accomplishments only made the verbal abuse worse, and for a year, I spent it dimming my light to support and please him. It was never good enough. *I* was never good enough. And he let me know every chance he could.

His charm was so beguiling that he had my *entire* family fooled. He hated and tried to isolate me from my best friend because God forbid someone actually encourage or support me. I'd always been the type of woman who proudly said it would never be me until it became me, and for two and a half years, I fucking hated the person I changed into trying to please someone who just wanted to control how I felt about myself.

The second I got myself a good divorce attorney, I filed for divorce, but by then I had gotten promoted to director of my department and was the breadwinner. Because we hadn't signed a prenup, in a last effort to hurt me, he found a decent enough lawyer to fight for his right to alimony because he knew that even with my promotion, I couldn't survive living in the city paying him hundreds of dollars a week. So, in an attempt to keep my job, I moved in with my aunt in Newark for three years until I was in a better financial situation. I literally only stopped paying that asshole a year and a half before my reconnection with Evan because he had finally decided to ruin some other woman's life by remarrying.

After that I told myself I was *never* going to put myself in that situation again. I promised I would never be in a serious relationship again. I told myself this, and I told myself that. What I wasn't counting on was repeating some of the same steps with Evan and I was too scared to think about how he might change, because with men, they always do. At the end of my admission, Evan took a deep breath.

"I understand why you didn't share that with me. That was a lot." My stomach became a sinking stone, realizing that this was not the reaction I was expecting from him. I wanted the typical Evan fashion. The one where he would get angry, the one where he would get defensive. I needed the Evan that would just talk to me and tell me how he felt, because this quiet version, this tapped out Evan who barely had words for me was frightening. I didn't do so well with frightening.

"Papi, would you please say something?" I paced back and forth, a nervous wreck for that five minutes he hadn't said a word.

"You don't trust me?" Confused, my mouth dropped and my brows knitted together wondering how he came to that conclusion.

"What is that supposed to mean?" He stood his full height, raking his fingers through his rich, dark hair.

"I just knew that it had to be something. Something massive keeping you from being one hundred recent invested. I tried not to see it. I tried to show you how much I love you for what you are, who you are and what you will be. But the real issue isn't that you don't want to marry me. It's the fact that you don't trust that I would *never* put you through what your clown ex put you through. You're coming from a place of pain and hurt, but I thought..." He paused considering his words.

"I thought my love was healing you. The way yours healed me... I was wrong." He admitted, eerily calm, as tears formed in my eyes when he made it to the tents entrance. My heart pistoned against my ribcage, trailing behind him before he got a chance to get far. It didn't feel like he was just walking away from me. It felt like he was walking away from us.

"Where are you going?"

"Back to the retreat to pack my things. I don't need the rest of the trip to tell me that when we get home we have a hard decision to make. Since your cousin is just a few hours away, it's probably best if you get in contact and spend some time with her so we could both have a few days alone to come to terms with this. Just know if you come with me today we're having this conversation as soon as we get home. I'll leave it up to you what you decide."

CHAPTER FOURTEEN

Luz

My mind and heart were playing a tug of war of whether I had done the right thing. When it came to my decision-making skills, I don't know why I listened to either. Evan was on his way back home. We agreed that we had needed space from one another, so instead of cutting my trip short, I decided to visit Los Angeles for the duration of the time I'd taken off.

It was convenient to have family here, as I'm not sure a plane ride and taxi crammed together would have helped us. Even so, while I was excited to see my cousin's new stomping grounds, all the turmoil running through me was anchoring me down like a ship.

Evan needed time to process all that he had learned about my past. Naively, I thought I would never have to share a time so traumatizing for me, because I hadn't known how important marriage was to securing our future.

One thing that brought a sense of relief? He wasn't as upset as I thought he'd be. In fact, he wasn't mad at all, just disappointed. Not that that made me feel better, but I had been grateful for disappointment over anger. At a point so vulnerable for me, the last thing I needed was another reminder of what my past shitty partners had been like.

At least with disappointment, there came a place of trying to understand. Marriage was this big step people took lightly. For the sake of being married, especially as a woman, you'll often ignore blatant red flags because your feelings were intense. It was romanticized by what it *could* be, not what it actually was.

I'll be honest, when everything was good, there was this sense of accomplishment. Marriage was serious, and I think everyone went into it praying they'd be good at it, but considering I had survived one marriage already, it was an experience Evan and I did not share.

To me, marriage was an amplifier, not a deterrent. Good traits stayed good, but bad traits became worse. It was why I had wanted to live with Evan first, to see if we were even compatible enough to survive long-term under the same roof.

Sure, we got on each other's nerves on occasion, and I risked him becoming comfortable with not changing much about our relationship, but I would have rather had that outcome than to marry someone and learn that I fell in love with this stranger. Maybe after this weekend that's how he saw me. Wondering about all the things running through his mind right now, proved to be my greatest distraction because before I could process it, Mikayla was pulling up in her luxury convertible to drive me back into LA.

***

"Hey, baby cousin," I spoke in my most annoying voice as I made my way to her car. My cousin had this weird obsession with the color pink. I don't think I've ever seen her wear another color. As someone who spent their entire adolescent being on the emo/goth side I tried not to judge her adult compulsion to wear pink head-to-toe. She definitely knew how to make it look sophisticated and elegant. I'm sure that came from her days as a pageant queen because if anyone knew how to strut like they were walking on a runway, it was my prima Mikayla.

Reaching into hug her, she even smelled pink. You know, assuming whatever fragrance she was wearing was floral. There had been hints of a begonia or a hydrangea in there or something, but it was the perfect amount of spicy and feminine.

"I've missed you."

"Look at you being all soft. Nah, I'm just playing. I missed you, too. I really appreciate being able to stay with you, Evan and I just need a few days to consider things and it's hard to when you're all up under each other."

"You guys doing okay?" Knowing she wasn't asking for a complete rundown, just a detail or two to tame her curiosity.

"Not everything resolved itself the way we wanted. But now he knows why marriage meant different things to us. I feel like we're going to be okay if we just put in a little bit more work but for now we just need space," reminding her that I'd appreciate it if this stayed between us.

Before long, I was loading my bag into her trunk of her luxury vehicle. "I like your new car! Homegirl must be making that gwap," I teased.

"I do okay," as we buckled up, and Mikayla finally took to the road.

"So, what's on the agenda? What would you like to do first?"

"Huh?" I questioned. Mikayla mistook my confusion for an inability to hear, as she turned the radio down and reframed her question.

"Is this a shopping and get-our-hair-done kind of visit? Is it a brunch and mimosas kind of time? You're only here a couple days, so I want you to enjoy the trip."

As good as shopping sounded, I didn't know how they did things in LA. Most of my pieces were designer but only because of my job, so in times when I did shop for myself, I was used to haggling and I wasn't sure LA would be the right environment for that.

"All I know about California is: it doesn't rain in Southern California and that there's a hotel." Continuing on with all the cheesy quotes, lyrics and song titles I could think of in reference to the joke.

"When you first got here, what were some of the things first things you did?" Hoping to take some ideas from her.

"Well, it's different for me because I live here. I was trying to reinvent myself, so I tried a lot of things I wouldn't do back home. Some of them I'm not even comfortable sharing." She uncomfortably laughed.

"What are you doing out here? Let me find out my baby cousin out here playing tennis and getting flewed out by European billionaires—"

"I wouldn't say all that," she interrupted, hoping to change the subject. "How about we just get something to eat and we'll go from there." As if on command, my stomach rumbled, hoping to be taken care of.

"I could go for some food. They got Dominican restaurants out here, right?" I asked, getting nervous at Mikayla's lips suddenly stretched out into a thin line.

"Let me warn you now: the Latin scene on this side of the country is a bit different. The Caribbean Spanish speaking community is scarcer. Hence why the actual good Caribbean restaurants are few and far between," she confessed.

Fishing for the door handle on my end, I was confused when it wouldn't open. "You got a child knock on the door? I got to get out of here. You're telling me there ain't not *one* Dominican, Puerto Rican *or* Cuban restaurant in this state? I would even fuck with Jamaican. At least that's Caribbean—"

"Luz, calm down. I said that there may not be many *restaurants* that cater to our tastes that are close by, but there might be a food truck or two," Mikayla chimed in.

"Girl, please. Imagine me waiting in line at a food truck just to get traditional Dominican food in California."

***

"Wow, this food is *really* good." Which was saying a lot because I was devouring my food by the morsel. Damn, were the toothpicks edible, too? Since New York had way more Dominicans, I had never had to hit up a food truck serving up Yaroa, or Dominican street food more commonly served in Santiago, back in my parent's homeland.

I'm seeing that was a big mistake, while it didn't remind me of traditional plates found in a Dominican kitchen, it certainly served up flavorful food-on-the-go type options, that could impress a yuppie or someone close to the culture alike. Hopefully this truck was making bank, because California was suffering with limited Afro-Latin restaurant options.

I had opted for sandwich known as a chimi burger, the sazon-seasoned beef patty, topped with cabbage, tomatoes, and served on toasted French bread, but that wasn't even the best part about it.

The finishing touch was a pink chimichurri sauce, a mash up ketchup, mayonnaise, soy sauce, orange juice, and Worcestershire sauce, depending on the truck's access. There were fries made up of mashed yuca root and maduros, or fried sweet plantains. I was in heaven. When I was eating right, all my problems appeared small and fixable.

Since Mikayla was more familiar with the spot, it was her go-to that made her feel a little closer to home. You could tell from the recognition of the owners that they saw her face here every week or two. Especially the way they were hooking her up with the extras that I gladly benefitted from.

It was all brought together by enjoying everything in the park nearby. I don't know about Newark, her hometown, but I couldn't remember the last time a lunch break gave me enough time to walk to the park closest to the Modern magazine building and enjoy the serene atmosphere of nature, all while being filled up on good food. Not going to lie, I was envious she even *made* time for it, but I was happy she didn't neglect the small things that made you feel a little more sane.

"So...on a scale from one to ten, when it comes to *niceness*, how would you rate the people in LA in comparison to East Coasters?"

Mikayla took a bite from her food and pondered with consideration. "Hmm...New York and New Jersey a two, LA a nine. But take in mind, while they're nicer, what I will say is kindness is lacking here."

As a New Yorker, I totally understood what she was saying. New Yorkers would cuss you out, but still put a jacket on your baby. They might berate you for bumping into them by accident, but still proceed to walk you *three miles* to your destination when you admitted that you were lost.

According to Mikayla, in LA, most people were nice, so long as they didn't have to extend any help to you.

"That's obviously just *my* experience. Maybe others have had a completely different LA, but there's so much to do and so many opportunities. I don't see myself leaving California for a while," she confidently admitted.

That took me back a bit. Even though I liked to visit other places, I couldn't see myself living anywhere but New York. It would be a hard place to leave because everything...*everyone* I loved was there. Just when I thought my mind was off Evan, there he went finding more ways for me to miss him. Maybe it would be a good idea if we did something fun.

"So where to next?"

CHAPTER FIFTEEN

Evan

Sometimes I wish there was an off switch, where I could just turn off my negative thoughts all at once. The only positive thing was that everything was out in the open now, but I still wasn't sure how I felt about it.

Luz, the love of my life, had been married before and it shaped her entire opinion on why she didn't want to do it again. Luz's experiences had exposed our differences, and those said differences shaped her opinion on things beyond my control. But unlike bias and misogyny, topics that in our time together I had learned to look at objectively, I didn't know how to unlearn not wanting to be married to that special someone. While I wasn't super religious anymore, the Catholic upbringing in me hadn't wanted to disappoint my practicing parents.

Not that I was marrying for them; marriage had always been one of those life goals I put off until I got my shit together. If it were up to my mother, I would have been hitched by thirty but even then, I wasn't where I am now financially. I took pride in knowing that I had been waiting to do it the right way for *me*. But it didn't mean that deep down, I still sought out her approval for big decisions like this.

Nothing would have made my folks happier than announcing our upcoming engagement, especially since I had thought about going up to see them now that I had a few days off. It was time we should have been spending at the retreat, but obviously *that* hadn't blown over well. The transit from the plane to our penthouse all blended into a blur, as I anticipated relieving J.C. of his dog sitting duties.

For a generous fee, J.C. had offered to stop by and check up on our dogs, so that they can be properly washed and fed. It was usually something we recruited a neighbor for, but all my go-tos were out of town, or on vacation. Seeing how J.C. was on his winter vacation, he seemed more than happy to make a couple extra bucks.

Plus, I'm sure the limitless cabinets and a full refrigerator was a decent motivator. He had a seventeen-year-old metabolism, so he ate like a garbage disposal. As long as he enjoyed and cleaned up after himself, it wasn't a problem to make an extra grocery store stop before we left for California. Not expecting any other random visitors, I zoomed through the front door to learn J.C. had a guest.

"Hey," I said in a long drag.

The other kid looked close to J.C.'s age. When he stood to introduce himself, outside of height, there wasn't much that they had shared physically in common, side from them both being brown skinned.

"Sorry to surprise you." Receiving his firm grip of a handshake. "I'm J.C.'s friend, Fabian. We were hanging out when he decided to stop by and he didn't know how long it would take so—"

"No need to explain," I interrupted. "I wouldn't have wanted you to wait outside or anything. Plus, I didn't ask this of J.C. under the condition that he couldn't have a friend or two over. It's a penthouse. I get it." Laughing as I hung up my jacket on the coat rack.

"Hey, I just filled her water bowl and—" J.C. froze as he walked out from the hallway, surprised to see me so early.

"Oh, I didn't think you'd be back so soon," He uncomfortably looked from me to Fabian.

"I'm actually gonna go. It was nice hanging out, J.C.," he said before offering J.C. a modest handshake. He threw out one last 'Nice meeting you' before hightailing out of the door making me think that I had said something wrong.

"Nice kid," I said, pointing my thumb in the direction the door. "Everything okay? He seemed to be in a hurry to leave. I hope I didn't say anything to make him feel like he *had* to go."

"No, it was just getting late," J.C. defended. "It wasn't you or anything, I'm just sure he had to go."

"Well, how have you been the past few days? No one gave you any trouble stopping by, I hope."

Since some people in my building had rarely seen any of my kids, I put a lot of measures in place to ensure that no one would bother him or accuse him of breaking in. For my neighbors who would be home, I let them know that a friend of mine was stopping by and to resist the urge to call the cops. Even though I shouldn't have had to do it, before we left, Luz made it clear that unless I explained it in detail, there could be problems.

The multiple people filling in as concierge at the front desk were all well informed who would be coming to make sure our pets were walked and taking care of, a few hours a day. I even checked in once at the retreat to make sure that there had been no issues, but it didn't mean as much not coming from the horse's mouth.

"The front desk people remembered me from when you introduced me from before, so they never gave me any problems. Nice and helpful if I needed it. No lie though, some of your neighbors gave me some anti-Black vibes, but no one ever minded my business for me. I'm sure if they forgot what you told them or just assumed that I was related to Luz." Guess you having a Black girlfriend counts for something.

"Is there a reason you're back so early?" he asked, curiosity riddled in his tone. Having left his book bag on the couch, he started packing his stuff up, looking like he was on his way out. "Not that I'm trying to be in your business. I just didn't expect you until next Thursday."

Interesting thing was that I actually trusted my kids with my love life. If I hadn't, I would have never gone on that speed dating event and met Luz. It just didn't feel like a place I wanted to put either of them in to be a rehabilitation center for my emotional labor, so I assured him things were fine and that Luz was just visiting family in LA.

"Do the dogs need to eat or walk at all?"

"I literally just fed them. They were a little easier to handle when it came to walking them with help. Hence why I suggested Fabian come to chill. Plus, he's never gotten to chill in the penthouse before."

It would be a while before Miss Mary Mack or Carmelo bothered anyone, as everything I had planned to take care of upon arriving home were all done. "You didn't leave me much to do," I joked. "Think you'd like to stick around and throw the ball around for a little while?"

J.C.'s face soured into a cringe. "Nah, it's too brick for all that. But I'd settle for that versus. See you've got that new one, but I don't want to impose if you hadn't gotten the chance to get your fill of it yet."

"Okay, set that shit up." Boastfully challenging him, as I excused myself to put my luggage away. By the time I returned, J.C. had his game of choice and two controllers at the ready, making me regret challenging a teenager with no bills and the ability to gain nothing but raw experience since he didn't have a nine-to-five job to go to.

Video games had always been Luz's thing. Despite getting into classic VS games and 2K, she tossed around words like Final Fantasy, Kingdom Hearts, RPGs, pretty much foreign terms when you were only used to Street Fighter and Mortal Kombat.

"Come on, let me get up the daze," J.C. hilariously yelled, as I finally bested him for the first time, resulting in my first K.O. of twelve rounds.

"What I lack in skill, I make up for in patience. You get sloppy and predictable once you get cocky." Something that had him rolling his eyes just as much as the first time I'd said it to him at fifteen.

J.C. sneered at me with that look of disgust that I had learned from Luz was less about being revolted and more of a reaction often used for feeling played. "Damn, the least you could do is serve ya boy some hot cocoa or something. The way you talking, I'm starting to feel a little unwelcome," he challenged, as we took a short break from the game.

We joined each other in the kitchen where nearly every cabinet in the kitchen had been raided of something, reminded me of those times when I was that age and ate everything in sight.

"Evan, I was wondering if there was something that I could ask you about if you didn't mind listening?" He spoke with hints of nervousness and hesitation in his tone.

"J.C., you know you can come to me with anything. School stuff. Basketball stuff," I replied as I dumped the cocoa contents in one of Luz's Adventure Time mugs, waiting for the water to reach a boil. "What if it's not about school or sports?" Asking it as if the subject matter brought him more anxiety than relief.

"I mean, it doesn't have to be related to school or sports. As long as it's not an alibi or anything," I joked, which didn't seem to change the mood in the air, making me regret the joking in the first place.

J.C. had always been one of the kids that wanted the most mentoring, so he was just a much as a friend as he was a kid I coached. If he needed an alibi, I probably would fill that need for him, so long as the situation was something he couldn't easily get himself out of.

Instead of sticking my foot in my mouth again, I let him approach starting the conversation on his own. Clearly, he needed that. "So, there's this person that I like. It's so new. I kind of feel like I'm overthinking it, sometimes." He shook his head in disappointment.

"I usually don't have major anxiety with the thought of dating someone. Real talk, dating is normally easy for me," he bashfully admitted, taking the prepared hot cocoa that I slid it across the table.

"You must really like the girl. I guarantee you, that's the main reason for your anxiety," I challenged before J.C.'s normally brown cheeks settled into a rusty ruddy hue.

"Actually . . . " He paused a considerable time to wonder whether he was making a mistake or not. "It's actually not a girl." Not being able to meet my gaze.

Suddenly his friend nervously excusing himself seemed to make more sense. "Oh, okay." Trying not to have a surprise reaction. "I'm assuming it was your friend Fabian?"

"Kinda." Pulling at the skin on the back of his hand. I understood his reluctance to share. Locker rooms could be toxic depending on the tolerance of the generation. Everything was becoming more acceptable, except for in things like sports and music.

"Have you shared this with anyone?" Hoping that he had at least shared it with someone in his peer group.

"No. Sometimes, I'm not even sure that I should. We're both on the basketball team and I just don't know how everyone's gonna take it."

From J.C.'s account, Fabian didn't have a strong support system as much as he did and couldn't afford to be outed. While he was being looked at by colleges, J.C. may have had a stronger system for support, but he was still ashamed to admit that he wasn't sure how his mom would react and whether she would be okay with him exploring his sexuality.

"I think I'm just afraid because I still like girls, but I want to be myself. I know some girls won't care either way. It's just, this feeling? I'm so busy trying to process it, but everything feels so unfamiliar to me."

This was really one of those times I wish Luz was here. It shouldn't have taken so long, but I was finally understanding her bi-ness and all the erasure and hyper-sexuality that often came with it. Growing up with conservative parents, this was *exactly* her experience. I wasn't the right person to confide in but he trusted me. I at least owed him the chance to try. "To be honest, dating isn't easy at any stage in a person's life. But I see how it's especially challenging, considering some teenage boys are never taught boundaries or anything other than exaggerated masculinity. That part I can at least relate to.

"When you're on a path to growth, you're probably gonna lose a lot of friends. That doesn't mean you can't meet new people who share the values you gain as you evolve. It's just gonna feel like you're the only one going through stuff, but no one's experience is so unique that another person won't experience something of that magnitude. That being said, do you like your friend enough to lose people?"

"That's the thing. I *do* like him, but putting it like that makes me even more nervous to tell people."

"I'm sorry, J.C. I probably should have worded it better. I should have asked are you ready to lose people who say homophobic, or in your case, biphobic things, even if it's just subtle shit? Because you have to be prepared that not every person in your life is meant to be there forever. Being yourself will always be worth the risk, but it may not always feel that way in that moment."

"I think I'm just afraid to tell people because I don't want anyone to treat me differently. Fabian, I get it, but I'm not sure I can wait until college to be...well, me."

J.C. still had some time to go before college and I was proud that with his PSAT scores, GPA, and grades, he had a lot of options for grants and scholarships. As the conversation shifted, J.C. admitted that he might not play in college, but I knew he was going to take advantage of his opportunity to go to college.

"I think there was this pressure put on me to consider going pro from family. Even though I'm good, I don't know if I'm good enough to damage my body that way. Plus, it worked out for you. You quit basketball and now you have like your dream life. Good job. Penthouse apartment. A bomb car. A fine ass girlfriend."

"Real talk, even though you're corny as fuck, you're still a huge inspiration to me. Thinking I could be that someday to other Black and Puerto Rican kids? I don't know, I just want to be someone's inspiration. Not that I'm trying to be all mushy about it," J.C. tried to quickly dismiss.

"Yeah, you don't have to worry about that J.C. I kind of tuned everything out after that corny as fuck comment." Which was a lie. I processed everything he'd said and even though at times I felt a bit undeserving of it, I'm just glad one day there might be a someone like me for kids, that actually looked like the kids that they were mentoring. That sounded awesome.

Even though we said we weren't going to be mushy, I still asked him for a hug because seeing my kids evolve made me feel like a proud parent, and I wasn't about all that toxic-masculine-can't-hug-another-guy type shit.

"Cue in the Uncle Jesse music," J.C. joked, making me wonder how someone his age even knew that reference.

"And now you ruined it." Joking back, giving him a light tap on the shoulder. When my phone started to ring, like a thirsty motherfucker, I rushed toward it, hoping it was Luz.

It wasn't.

"Hey, Ma."

"Evan, my boy. How are you?" My mom, a boastful tone to her voice.

"Fine, I guess. Any reason for the call?" I knew that if my mom was calling, it had taken me too long to check in with her during the week. With the retreat and our relationship problems, I'd had too much on my mind to do a weekly check in with my folks.

"I need a reason to call my only son?" Before going off into a tirade of how long she had been in labor with me and that enough should have granted her the respect that I wasn't giving her.

I know, dramatic.

"Anyway, I was going to the city tomorrow and wanted to know if you'd be around for lunch. It'd be nice to see you on more than just the holidays."

"Sure, Ma." I replied, solidifying our plans until it felt appropriate to admit that I had to go since I had company.

"Damn, Ma Dukes was going in on that ass. That was painful watching a grown ass man get cussed all by his mom. I'm seeing Italian moms ain't that much different from Black-Puerto Rican ones."

In all fairness, my boys had never *seen* my mom resting in her true personality. I don't know how she had managed to trick every single one of them in believing she was Gramma Nutt from Candyland, but I didn't always get that sweet old lady bit. No wonder J.C. was surprised that you're never too old with an Italian mom.

"I'm kinda all video game-d out now, but if you don't have to immediately go home, I can order some ramen and we could watch one of those shows that you're always trying to put me up on."

"I mean, if it's your treat, then hell yeah," J.C spurted before I excused myself to go to the bathroom. I just needed a minute. I didn't want to be my myself, but it was stressing me out that Luz still hadn't reached out. My phone lingered in my hand, my fingers gliding over the screen at the contact *Baby*.

We had only been separated a day, and I already missed her like crazy. A deep sigh didn't erase my problems, but it did provide a temporary relief. Should I just call her to see how she's doing? No, I didn't want to ruin her time with her cousin, especially since she didn't see her often.

Pulling myself together, I rubbed the frustration off my face and exited out the contact screen. Dialing a number to the spot Luz and I frequented, I made my way back to the living room to confirm what J.C. wanted and was told the wait time would be twenty minutes. I was finally feeling the distance between Luz and me, and it fucking sucked.

CHAPTER SIXTEEN

Evan

"Hello, gorgeous." I approached my mother from the side, interrupting her window shopping. At the sight of me she rolled her hazel eyes, irritation lining her sharp features. In an effort to get to the restaurant, I nudged her away from her current spot, but of course she had words for the subject of her curiosity.

"This place here, they opened a shop where people can play board games now? And people actually pay to do that?" I'd never been a nerd, nor have I ever taken an interest in board games, but with the neighborhoods demographic changing, you saw a lot of the newer shops catering to yuppies and transplants. I wasn't originally from the boroughs but my dad was and while my mom was a Jersey native, she navigated the city like a pro.

"Yeah, Ma, I know. Lots of useless shops. Can we get going? I want to beat the lunch hour rush," I said, gripping my hands on her shoulders and guiding her in my desired direction. Oftentimes, I forgot how short my mom was, especially when we were walking around the city and she opted for her more comfortable shoes.

"I tell you, you can't even fear getting robbed in this neighborhood anymore. Everywhere you go there's a Lululemon. The last time I was here it used to be all Puerto Rican. Or is it Afro Latino? I always get those two confused," she admitted shamelessly. "I swear there's more White people living here than Denmark right now. I feel like I'm not even in the same Williamsburg anymore. I used to love coming here."

"Ma, lower your voice," I said, knowing my mom's brand of political incorrectness wouldn't be everybody's cup of tea, however, I was proud she preferred the area in its past existence, as underserved as it was. For my mom, culture was everything, so to see her torn by the wonders of yester years made me certain some of her ignorant views were changing. Even if it was at a snail's pace.

"Your father used to take me to this corner shop that used to be right *there*." She pointed across the street to what now stood a yoga studio and plant shop. "The owner was so good to us. They'd sell us salami this big for ten bucks." Her arms stretched wide emphasizing the size of the salami in her story. "I wonder how much money they offered him to sell his place. I hope it was for a lot for what's there now. Ten bucks. *Sheesh*. The only thing you can get here now for ten bucks are directions. I don't know how you and Luz do it. That would drive your father and I crazy." It was only a matter of time before she mentioned Luz. As much as I wanted to vent about it, I prayed she didn't press me. Being bad at lying was something that worked in her favor and I just wanted a nice little winter date with my mother.

"This is it, Ma." We stood outside the restaurant, a small line already forming since it was close to lunchtime. She adjusted her purse over her shoulder throwing a side eye my way.

"I can't believe I let you talk me into a mac and cheese place. There should only be one type of macaroni and cheese and that's a classic cheddar." I placed a kiss on her cheek, knowing when she was in a nagging mood like this, it was her chill mode and when the line moved at a faster than normal pace, before I knew it we were inside and directed to be seated.

"I'm guessing you and Luz come here a lot, huh? Where is she anyways? I wanted to know how she's liking that hair mask I sent her a few weeks ago. The girl at the counter recommended it for people with that curly hair she has, but if she doesn't like it they have a thirty-day return policy. I can get her something else." It just figures my mom would spend the afternoon bringing up the one topic I was trying to forget. Luz this. Luz that. You would think the name Luz was synonymous with her son now.

"Uhhhh...Ma, she's away visiting family." I eased my coat off and laid it in the space beside me as my mom fluffed out her feathered hair in the reflection of a napkin holder.

"Back to her mom's home country?"

"No, Ma. California. She's got a cousin out there," I replied, taking the menu to pretend to decide what I would order knowing I had already planned to get the Gouda and bacon bowl. The spinach and parmesan bowl had always tempted me since the one time I'd tried it, but there was something about bacon that always made my go-to choice a clear winner. It was my mom who needed more time deciding. Ignoring a comment about how skinny I looked and whether or not Luz was feeding me, when the waitress returned to take our order I smiled and let her try to sell me on dishes I'd already tried before just to shift the conversation off Luz.

"Do you need a little more time sweetheart?" she asked, and my mom surprised me when she wasted no time by ordering the goat cheese bowl, something I didn't even know she liked until now.

"Hey, Mom, I didn't know you liked goat cheese."

"Son, there's a lot of stuff you don't know about me. You think I tell you everything," she spat. Had to love Italian moms. Taking a sip of my artisan soda to kill the awkward silence, I wondered why my dad didn't come. Early March was always his favorite time to drive down since my uncle Rocco shared a birthday with him and often, they would spend it together.

"Hey, why didn't Dad come? Is he too busy with the restaurant? I know he's glad to be fully operational again, but I thought he was talking about hiring another guy to run a place so he didn't have to be there every day."

"Oh, you know your father is stubborn as a mule. He talked about it but I don't know, I don't think he's cut out for retiring. All he knows is work. I don't know what he'd do if he were at home bothering me all day. The restaurant is practically his life. You know that. He wanted to come, though. He loves to see you coach those kids."

"I was just actually hanging with one the other day. That kid is going places."

"You should bring them over for dinner again. Although maybe when your cousin Berto isn't there. You know he's got those strong opinions, if you know what I mean." Yeah, I knew what she meant all right. He was a full-on bigot and didn't even try to hide it. If I knew ahead of time he was showing up I always made an excuse to spend certain holidays with Luz's family. My kids had it hard enough.

"That one year you brought them I swear, it was the first time we never had leftovers. Unbelievable. Now those are some young boys that appreciate a home cooked meal. Although it did make me kind of grateful we didn't have more sons, the way you ate. I'm surprised we were able to send you to college."

With lightning speed, the waitress returned with our orders and after a short grace, my mouth was met with the gooey tenderness of Gouda cheese and the savory guilty pleasure of bacon. Mac and cheese was that comfort food I couldn't explain why I loved so much stuff since my mom didn't grow up making it. But every time I had it, my guarded exterior came down and my overall mood was far more forgiving. It had to be the way a woman felt after downing a whole bowl of ice cream after a breakup. Although the plan was to keep the conversation light, I couldn't help wanting advice from the woman who has yet to steer me wrong. Relaxing in my seat, I rested the spoon in my bowl, preparing for a hard conversation and an even tougher opinion.

"Ma, I've been wanting to ask you something." Adjusting her glasses on her nose, her defined eyebrows furrowed meeting me with a worried look.

"You know, you don't know how much you look like your father when you do that face. That doom face. I hate it when you do that." Taking a deep breath, I pushed through knowing it would only annoy her if I dragged it out.

"When Dad asked you to marry him, what made you say yes?" As if the question caught her off guard, she laughed as she reached for a napkin to wipe stray green onions from the corner of her mouth.

"Well, you're older now so let me see if I can help make you understand. Your grandfather is sweet now but when I was younger, he was a *mean* drunk. I really just wanted a way out my parents'house, so at the time marrying your father felt like a certain type of freedom. Only getting married turned out to be another prison I wasn't prepared for. So, the reason I said yes was just the lesser of two evils." Swirling the ice in my glass, my brows shot up at her confession. Here I was thinking it was because she loved my dad.

"You thought being married to Dad was a prison?"

"Well, not a *real* prison but you know, not the freedom I thought it'd be. I had all these dreams of becoming independent and successful. I wanted to go to medical school."

"Well, why didn't you?" Her face softened, giving me this sympathetic look like I had just lost a fight.

"Because I had you. Besides having a husband in my day was like having another son. I prioritized my family because that's what people did when we were young. I hope you're not listening to this and hearing that I don't love my life. I've always loved my life. I've also always loved your father. But I think if I had grown up in your time, who knows what I'd be doing right now." She shrugged. Growing up I always looked at my parents having a semi-perfect relationship. A couple I aspired to be like one day. My folks never excessively fought, had never made each other feel small, and while they weren't openly affectionately like I'd be with my future wife, you didn't have to be around them long to feel their love for each other. Was there something behind the scenes I just didn't see?

"Ma. I asked Luz to marry me." Her bright eyes widened, her bracelets jingling when her elbows met the table.

"Well, don't leave me in suspense. Did she say yes?" Rubbing my forehead, I took another deep sigh.

"No, she didn't. Honestly, I don't even know where we are right now. Ma, truth is, Luz is away visiting her cousin but only *after* I left her there. We've been having some problems so she talked me into this couples' retreat. Long story short, we walked out with more problems than we came in with. I just felt like we needed the time away from each other. But now... now I'm not so sure." She pushed her glasses further up her nose bridge, speechless. Maybe even disappointed.

"How do I know I did the right thing?" Pushing her bowl off to the side she interlocked her fingers and released a heavy sigh. I was going to get her take whether I wanted to hear it or not.

"Honey you don't. In the moment and right after you've had the time to think about your decisions, always feel like two different right things. Do you know why she said no?" In all fairness to Luz, I chose not to disclose the why. I didn't want to be talking about it in the first place, and it wasn't my truth to tell. I did end up telling her that she would be back in a few days, though.

"Evan, you know I'm always on your side. No matter what you do, no matter what you say. I'm always gonna support you." And this was where I knew a big *but* was coming on.

"But is it marriage itself? Or is it just *you* she doesn't want to marry, because those are two different assessments." I shook my head.

"Well, she sold her condo to move in with me. And we just adopted another dog together. Plus, it was her idea to get counseling, so it isn't just me. People fall in love with each other and want to get married, isn't that how it's supposed to work?"

"In our day, yes, but sweetheart, sometimes you kind of live in this fantasy. You always have, Evan. You were everything your father and I raised you to be. Caring, attentive, thoughtful and generous, but you're also a man with high expectations. Expectations I'm not sure just anyone can meet for you. When I was young, men didn't have to be *likable* to get the woman of their dreams. They just had to have a job. Even better if you were just *kind of* handsome and responsible. Women today don't really need men like we used to. So, if a woman actually *likes* you, the way that girl loves you, sometimes you just have to cut your losses."

I couldn't believe what my mother was saying. All my life I had been led on one path. The one where I made my Catholic parents proud and followed my traditional values. In a perfect world, I knew my folks saw me ending up with a nice Italian girl. And as nice as that would have been, my relationship with Luz made me forget about shared culture, race, or the need to share the same values. All I saw when I looked at her was the love of my life. And I left her in California because things weren't shifting in my favor. That was not what you did when you loved someone. That's not what I should have done.

"Dear, take it from me. Men struggle more in relationships when things aren't easy because women spend so much time trying to make it look simple. We're Catholic, so there's nothing I want more than to see you walk down the aisle. But I'm also humble enough to admit that often, my views don't always age well in this new era where people have more choices and identities and types of relationships we didn't have thirty years ago. The other day I was watching Dr. Phil interviewing couples in polyamorous marriages and I go, where the hell were those when I wanted two husbands? You kids have everything now."

My mom's advice wasn't something I wanted to hear, but I definitely needed to. If I wanted something simple, it may have just been easier to get a blow-up doll. The real, the hard, the beautiful was everything I already had with Luz. Maybe she would change her mind in the future but pressuring and guilting her to relive trauma was only pushing her away. And I didn't want to lose her.

"Darling, she could have just walked away at any moment. But she chose to put in the work. Now I wouldn't go around bragging that y'all are out there seeing therapists but if it were me and your dad, I'd do anything to fix us. I think that's just what Luz was trying to do." I hated how she was always right. Taking my phone out of my pocket, I booked the next evening flight back into Los Angeles, something that made my mom blissfully happy. She wanted grandkids soon and didn't want me to waste another five years trying to get serious with another woman. I only wanted one woman and by this time tomorrow night, I was going to win her back.

CHAPTER SEVENTEEN

Luz

"Girl, I don't know whether I can go on there with absolutely *no* makeup on. Ya girl gotta have some lip stain or some brow pencil or *something*," I argued, fearing what I would look like on screen without makeup.

Mikayla usually batched her content, managing to fit her weekly YuVube content in the span of two days. The rest of her working week consisted of being in the field when it came to coaching women and femmes on habitual dating habits they needed to break.

Since I was a surprise guest, she wanted to make her scheduled live stream more interesting by doing a Get Ready with Me featuring her ultra-cool cousin, me. We had a little makeup counter set up on the floor, but I argued to the death about at least having great eyebrows if people were going to have to look at me.

"Come on, the point is to beat your face *on* camera, so people can see the products you're using. I'm trying to take advantage of all these shades that don't fit me because sometimes these companies send me shades or shadows that are too light for me, but perfect for you. You have to be willing to strip down," she asserted.

Easy for her to say; she had such great skin. Tell me why I got sunburned my second day here not knowing that I should have packed sunscreen.

This no humidity thing took me for a loop since back home when it was seventy degrees it *felt* like ninety. California on the other hand, had this *amazing* dry heat that would have you sitting out in the sun forever without feeling like it was scorching.

"We've got about ten minutes before everything starts, so I just want you to be prepared. The live stream usually starts out with me waiting for enough people to show but I'll probably start with introducing you as my guest. Don't be surprised if I do it again from time to time for people dropping in late. Every time you apply a product, try to make it as visible as possible, so the audience can see it." She demonstrated by holding up a foundation to her face with presenter-like charisma and went on to describe the product without sounding fake or oversell-y.

"So, can I say anything?" Regretfully wiping my natural look off with a makeup removing wipe, freeing my face of product.

"Every month, I answer about sixty to ninety minutes worth of questions. People who follow me but can't afford my rates for the coaching, I give them a chance to get quick advice. Things that can help them today, not big lifestyle changes, ya know?"

Mikayla explained that with a more privileged client, she would guide them on how to move during each stage of dating before becoming official, how to present themselves and how to leave men wanting more.

Even though I would never pay someone for her kind of service, I secretly envied not having the tips she picked up on her journey of learning how to date.

Neither one of our moms, Demeter included, had taught us how to properly date. Most of what Noelia, Mikayla's mom, used to spout was just how to be a perfect wife for a man. Being single was better than being with someone who stressed you out all the time, but one of the benefits of being with Evan was—*shit*.

I was getting ahead of myself. I wasn't sure what fate had in store for us when I returned back to New York. It was best not to complete that thought, otherwise, I'll be stressing myself about it all day.

"I hope people don't be asking crazy shit, like *I'm currently dating a man who I think has a wife but I love him. Should I leave him?*" I joked.

"Try not to laugh if people do. Sometimes people don't really want help. They just want to see if your answer will align with what they were already planning to do. I try not to judge anyone in their journey to be partnered since it gets the message across better."

See, that was the difference between me and Mikayla. If the questions were ridiculous, the city girl in me felt compelled to say something. "Girl, Imma try," trying not to give up my composure. Before I felt fully prepared, Mikayla's livestream was starting.

Mikayla started out like most influencers did, thanking everyone for coming and that if you join now, some things might sound repetitive since she planned to repeat information in the case people showed up later than others.

"Welcome all you beautiful people. If you are happening to stop by randomly, my name is Mikayla Morales and you know me from my platform Date like a Unicorn. Most of you already know but if you don't, I host monthly livestreams to offer advice to those who don't have the resources yet to budget for my dating coach services. Today's livestream is being sponsored by Fenty Beauty." She held her hand over the mini makeup counter we created on the floor, presenting it like Vanna White on an episode of Wheel of Fortune.

Even though a few stragglers jumped on and off, Mikayla was averaging about thirty-thousand users tuning in. From the point of a vertical writer, those are some impressive stats.

"I'm sure all of you are wondering who my guest is for today," Mikayla started before introducing me as her cousin from New York. I don't know why, but knowing thirty-thousand people were staring at me right now was flaring up my anxiety.

"That's right, I'm Luz De Los Santos, Mikayla's mature and hoe-positive magazine-writer cousin," I flirted to the camera, faking my confidence. "Today, I will be joining her for her get-ready-with-me. Maybe even give alternative objectives to y'alls questions."

Mikayla gave a disclaimer that any advice given might feel like a hard truth when you were resistant to improvement. But she reminded her audience that all she wanted was for those tuning in, to find the right partners for them.

What she didn't promise was that she could make those said relationships work once you found the partner or partners right for you. All successful relationships took work and required a different skill set to maintain.

Damn, it sounded like she should team up with a guru like our retreat counselor. She prepares you for the relationship and he helps you maintain it. Not trying to sound like a capitalist but that sounds like a collaboration in the making.

The longer I had the ring light on me, the more comfortable I got pretending that it wasn't there. Real talk, though? I don't think I've *ever* put on makeup so fast. By the time we were a half hour in, off and on, close to fifty-thousand users had stopped by. Maybe that was modest for some, but Mikayla didn't talk much about her work so I wasn't aware of how popular dating coaches could be.

"Look at this highlighter," Mikayla flirted into the camera. "I've always felt the more captivated a person is by your eyes, the more captivated they'll be by you. Small tip for makeup users," she continued on, letting me pick the next question.

Chile, I was successfully trying to keep my ass from laughing as the only thing getting me through, was hoping all these problems women had couldn't *all* be real. The first two or three Mikayla had chosen had been pretty tame, never deviating from trying to find balance between looking for a partner and having a social life and career.

My guess was, with the way Mikayla answered, some of that had to have come from her own lived experience, so I'm sure the advice were probably words at one point she had needed to hear herself.

The next question on the other hand, looked like it was straight out of a avoid-these-damn-dusties account and all I kept hoping was that some poor woman wasn't actually putting up with this.

"Hi, I am a beautiful in shape woman with no children. I have a successful career, which has given me the privilege of owning my own assets, such as my home and a car. I still crave a provider and have been taking the advice of some of these male dating gurus because to some degree, I feel like they give good advice and I find that both can provide good feedback to attract the man I want." *Girl, that was your first mistake.*

"Recently, I went on a date with someone who I vibed well with. High earner, good-looking, physically, my type. But I made it clear that I wasn't having sex until things were serious. He then proceeded to say that I should pay my own way on this, and future dates, because we shouldn't be bartering sex for getting to know someone.

"It feels like, because I said I wouldn't have sex, he's resentful and trying to punish me. Should I have just kept my mouth shut? Should I move on?" I put down Mikayla's iPad, trying to wash the taste of that situation out my mouth with my sparkling water nearby.

I didn't know what Mikayla was about to tell her, but I hoped it was in the lines of get-the-hell-outta-there.

"Well, you weren't wrong for stating your boundaries," Mikayla countered, doing her best to answer the user's question.

"But one thing we can all do better is invoke the art of listening," she said while pointing to her ear.

"When you're seeking a partner, especially a cisgender man, practicing the art of listening is your wisest tool. Let a person talk if you want to know their intentions. Don't worry if you feel like you're not getting asked much because you are auditioning *him*, don't let it be the other way around. My advice to you would be to move on if you prefer a more generous partner. This man doesn't sound generous. He can be everything you want, but if you're not comfortable with fifty-fifty, allowing it now will be a burden for tomorrow.

"Oftentimes, I see that fifty-fifty only comes up when it comes to finances. This is not a good or bad thing, but men are taught to value money or things that they have to *work* for or have to earn.

"If you can honestly live with going fifty-fifty until you're willing to be intimate, I can't tell you what to do, but it sounds like you're looking for a provider and he made it clear that unless sex is on the table, he has little interest in you or working for the main thing he wants from you." Wrapping up the question and moving on to another one.

The next question was just as chaotic, as Mikayla had to navigate giving advice to a woman who felt like her boyfriend was giving her an ultimatum for wanting to prioritize marriage in a relationship. For someone Mikayla's age, I was surprised that she was so good at this. Maybe I should have been taking her up on all those free advice sessions during her startup years.

"Next question, how can you tell when a man values you? Hmm...This one has both a long and short answer," she warned.

"The short answer is, when you're being taken care of, you never have to ask if someone is valuing you. Most men don't value with words, they show they value you with actions. Does your partner cook and then leave everything for you to clean? Because if he does, he values the time he spent cooking *more* than the time he expects you to clean his mess. If you're a stay at home partner, does he allow you time to yourself after most of your time was spent maintaining all his normals? Most people aren't conscious of the things around the house they need that seem small to *them*, because they don't provide that labor."

Mikayla later went on to give a short list of examples of things partners do when they actually care about you but not wanting to focus too long on the question, I wish that she'd stayed on topic because once she brought up the marriage aspect, everything felt real *loud*.

"I don't subscribe to the notion that women are easy, but look at it like this. Most people, regardless of gender, are not going to turn down something convenient for them. For some that might be a relationship where everything is split down the middle. Some situations might be intimacy without titles. Marriages are not an end-all-be-all but I always stress that marriage, while for some, it seems like a piece of paper, it's also your protection.

"People will absolutely sign a piece of paper for that property deed that they're not sure is a good location for their business. They'll also sign a loan agreement, a car note and a birth certificate, all things that could potentially cost them money.

"No one can guarantee a marriage won't fail, but men protect things and people they value. Marriage is an exchange. Maybe it's an exchange that some don't want to deal with but you're sacrificing the most because you will no longer have access to other partners unless you're polyamorous or in an open relationship. Your partner should *want* to protect you legally, as much as they do financially, physically and emotionally."

That was a perspective I had never considered. Maybe I've been looking at marriage through the eyes of someone who failed at it and not through the eyes of someone who has a partner willing to do all those things.

The first time I got married, dude was straight up broke and I was resentful having to Build-A-Bear. I let the idea of marriage become associated with my experience with him. Evan didn't need me to build him or provide anything that we couldn't do together. Our relationship wasn't equal but there were times he provided eighty percent when I only had twenty to give. It definitely didn't account for the times I gave seventy-five percent and to let him catch up, I let him only bring twenty-five.

Maybe he would change but I've known Evan for a really long time. He only ever changed for the better, why was I not trusting him based on my past with someone else? *Luz, baby, what is you doing?* Your ass needed to go back home...yesterday.

The things I needed to say couldn't be said through text or phone call. Not wanting to interrupt or break character during Mikayla's live stream, I waited until it came to an end to blurt out, "I think I'm making a mistake."

Confused, Mikayla asked me to backtrack before explaining that the last piece of advice she gave was right on the money and it wasn't just for the listeners. "I have to go. I'm probably making things worse by wasting all this time making it seem like I don't care about him—"

"Luz, take a beat," Mikayla interrupted. "Leaving now will only make you stressed. Being stressed makes you say things without clarity. If you still feel that way in the morning, by all means go, but you two love each other, right?"

"Of course." I said, not knowing where those falling tears were coming from.

"Then stay until you have a clear head. You want to say the *right* words not the fast ones." Look at my cousin acting all wise. She probably got that shit from me.

"You're right." Falling back on the floor, defeated. "I just really want to tell him I'm sorry."

"Trust me, if you exercise patience, he'll be a *lot* more susceptible to hearing it."

CHAPTER EIGHTEEN

Luz

"Hey, Sleeping Beauty. Rise and shine." I woke up to my deranged cousin attacking me with a pillow. She wasn't light with her blows either. If I hadn't buried myself under the blanket to duck for cover, the hoe would have never stopped. This was a girl who did *not* know how to sleep in. Every morning if you weren't up by eight thirty, it was too bad because she didn't play that.

"Come on Mikayla. I literally have just days left on vacation. Plus, I'm still not adjusted to this time difference. Don't you see I'm tired as fuck?" When I poked my head out the covers all I saw was Mikayla decked up to the nines, a pink body con dress hugging her slender curves like she was going on a date. Her back long braids were arranged in a half up, half down array of sleekness, and her sky-high heels were definitely made for walking. A person who didn't know her would think she was doing something fancy but this was just everyday Mikayla. The girl would wear a cocktail dress to a grocery store. I loved looking nice too but was known to throw on a pair of Evan's sweat pants and a dirty sweater out of the hamper when I was in a rush. Mikayla would never.

"Fine, lazy bones, then I won't bother you. But just wanted to let you know I have a plumber coming in a little while to fix the kitchen sink. Do you mind straightening up the kitchen a little before he comes?" She asked, as I groaned in frustration.

"Kayla, are you serious?" She put her hands on her hips, in a way that reminded me of how my mom used to look at me when she would ask me to wash the dishes, and like a smartass I'd leave the spoons and forks out by technicality. Only Mikayla was my height and from this bed looked like a fifty-foot woman trying to stomp on an ant.

"It's not like you didn't help me junk it up!"

"*Okay*, that's the cost of being a good host sometimes. When you come to visit me in New York, I promise, I got you." Without warning, she walked over to the closed blinds and pulled them back to let unnecessary light in. If I was back home it would be six A.M. and dark outside.

"Luz, porfa. It's only going to take you a few minutes and it doesn't have to be right now. If you do, I'll bring you back some food from the food truck," she singsonged. She was lucky I wasn't well adjusted to all the fast food Mexican spots out west. I did actually like Mexican food but I hadn't prepared myself for the fact that Caribbean restaurants weren't really a thing in California. The East Coast had really spoiled me. I needed my habichuelas and mangú stat.

"*Fine*. I'll straighten up when I'm up." She sat on the bed and gave me the biggest hug, damn near messing up my bonnet.

"Thank you, prima. Make sure you don't forget, okay? And brush your teeth, mama. There's a lot going on there." That I turned around for.

"Bitch, are you leaving or not?" She flipped her braids over her shoulder and grabbed her clutch on the vanity nearby.

"I'll be back in a couple of hours. And don't forget that second one. You'll thank me later," she added before she saw herself out. I thought being a neat freak was the one thing she hadn't inherited from my Titi Noelia, a woman known for her adjusting picture frames and dinner tables the right way or she'd have a fit. Nope, she was still her mother's daughter in all the ways that counted.

After having a round with my pillow and not being able to find the right groove, I figured it was the best time to get up and get it over with. What was it? A couple of dishes in the sink and wiping down a few counters? Once I finished I could hop right back into bed and be the bum I intended to be. Slipping on a pair of slippers I marched into the hallway and almost jumped out of my skin when I saw someone that was clearly *not* Mikayla sitting on the living room couch. At my scream he turned around and stood. It was Evan.

"Are you okay?" he asked, as I paused to catch my breath. I should have known my cousin was up to something. Now I know why she told me to brush my teeth.

"Yeah, I was just surprised to see you. Here I am thinking I'm all alone and poof, a man is sitting on the couch out of nowhere." If there was one thing my man knew how to wear, it was a damn Henley. *I mean*, if he was still my man after today.

"Your cousin let me in." He gestured toward the front door. He was wearing a baseball cap he'd adjusted from the back to front and looked far more rested than I was. Observing the perfectly spotless kitchen, it was obvious my cousin was only trying to get me out of the bed to prepare me for this.

"Do you have a few minutes to talk? I know things are really weird right now, but I had to get something off my chest." I nodded, remembering that I was in my bonnet, a torn t-shirt and shorts that I wouldn't dare wear to bed if I was trying to get laid. Aww man, was that my breath humming like that? I had to brush my teeth *ASAP*.

"Do you mind if I brush my teeth first? There are some things I want to talk about, too. I was going to wait until I got home but now that you're here, it doesn't make sense to wait."

Fidgeting with his hands, he asked if I wanted him to wait on the couch, but not knowing when Kayla would return, I suggested him waiting for me in the guest room while I made a beeline to the bathroom.

I didn't stop at brushing my teeth, I took off my bonnet and separated the eight twists my hair was in to keep my curls manageable while I slept. My curls on display improved my bum-ass appearance, but damn, were my eyes really that puffy? I was about to have the single most important conversation in my life and I had puffy skin and enough crust in my eyes to make a whole damn pizza. And then there was those pesky upper lip hairs. Sometimes I felt like a freakin' cat for how many whiskers I had thanks to PCOS. *Thanks a lot, genetics.*

A little pluck here, a little face wash there, and I was halfway decent to face the music. When I entered the bedroom, I found Evan looking at the family photos Kayla kept hanging on her vanity mirror.

"I like this picture of you." He huffed. "I feel like your mom has shown me every photo you've ever taken, so it's nice seeing one that's new to me. You look adorable. You always look adorable."

I had to be about fifteen in the picture. My hair had just gotten blow dried to death and at that point, if I had even heard the phrase "Voy a halar" again, I was going to take the blow dryer out of my mom's hand and shatter it to pieces. It was a wonder I didn't go natural then, but it *was* the reason I wasn't smiling in it. Evan turned to face me as I reached to take off his baseball cap. I assumed he was still upset with me since when I leaned into kiss him, he didn't kiss me back. He did however put his arm around me reminding me of how safe I felt in his embrace. I didn't want to lose that. I didn't want to lose him.

"What was that for?" he said in between kisses before he leaned in for another.

"Because I missed you." His smile was small but warm and his eyes shined the brightest green I'd ever seen.

"Thanks for brushing your teeth then." *Smartass*.

Placing my arms around his neck, he nuzzled his nose against mine and followed with a kiss on my forehead. "Come on, let's sit down." My heartbeat quickened at the thought of this conversation being the start or end to us. I had planned to write down everything I wanted to say to him on the trip home but being the procrastinator that I was, now I had no choice but to speak off emotion. It was times like this I wish I could predict just a fraction of the future.

When we sat down on the bed, I stroked his beard admiring how nice it looked after a few days of not trimming it like he usually did. "You look good, baby. You know I like it when it grows out a little." He took my hand, his emerald green eyes changing from whimsical to serious.

"Luz, let's stay focused, okay?" he replied, causing me to pout and lower my head. Meeting his gaze, whatever we were to discuss didn't look good.

"Okay." He brushed his thumb across my cheek and his lips pressed into a hard line.

"I wanted to talk about everything that's going on between us. Our relationship and where I stand." I took a huge gulp. Maybe it was a good thing that he went first.

"I wanted to wait until you got back but the time alone has given me some clarity, and I just couldn't wait. I've thought long and hard about this and I know this isn't going to work because neither one of us are willing to compromise." Fear settled in as I went into panic mode, ten seconds away from being on my knees to pleading with him.

"Evan, wait." He pressed his fingers to my lips.

"Luz. Please, just let me speak…" Tears formed in my eyes knowing this could be it. He was finally breaking up with me and

I for one, could not hold back tears long enough to even listen to where he was going with it.

"That's why I'm waving the white flag," he said, as I wiped the moisture from my eyes but couldn't control the sniffling that came with it. "When I got home my feelings were all over the place. I felt right in my decision on leaving but that first night without you was...it was empty. At first, I was just angry and by the time I came to my senses I just felt sad. I learned that without you this loneliness would be my forever. Because if I can't be with you, love is never going to feel the same. I know you hate being defined by relationships. I know you feel complete with or without me. But that's where I'm different. I'm not whole without you. And I couldn't wait another day to tell you that." Now I was crying again, but this time it was that ugly crying no one wanted to be caught dead doing in front of another person. Evan had that gift for words that often made me question if I even deserved him sometimes.

"I understand the way you look at marriage because I understand *you*. I don't see it through the same lens as you do but I just want to spend my life with you. This world isn't much of an existence without you because you are my world. It took leaving to help me see that." He helped me wipe away some of my tears but it was no use, they just kept coming. I was a mess.

"Luz, please stop crying. I hate seeing you cry." With an attempt to pull myself together, with my palms I wiped down my face and even got up to blow my nose. When I sat back down, everything I wanted to say had escaped me. There was nothing I could say to top his words of affirmation, so I went straight to my final speaking point. There was no need to waste any more time.

"Do you mind if I asked what the ring looked like?" I asked, while playing with the string of my shorts. From his pocket he pulled out a black velvet box, surprising me that he actually had it on him.

"I wasn't sure what to do with it. Because I got it custom, it's considered used, so that cancels out me getting back what I paid for it. Not sure why I kept it." He handed me the box, turning away from me as I popped the box open. The ring was beautiful. In a stunning gold frame, a diamond shaped heart as the main stone was accompanied by two rows of smaller stones in a modern twist design. It was exactly the ring I would have asked for if I'd known he had planned to propose and the inscription was going to send me back to a crying fit.

To Luz. The girl who changed me and the woman who loved me.

There was no way I could let this beautiful ring go to waste. My biggest fear of remarrying was the thought of a man having the power to diminish my light. Having to be all these things a partner expected of me while changing myself into something I didn't recognize in the process. Evan never expected that. With him, I shined brighter and he just loved me for me. All spoiled, confusing, goofy and flawed me. I just wanted to be a better partner for him. I wanted to be the wife that he wanted.

"Just curious, how would you have asked me?" He turned back to look at me, his elbows resting on his knees as he shrugged.

"Does it matter?" I closed the box and handed it back to him.

"Of course it matters. I just want to know." He rolled his eyes, dread weighing heavy on his masculine features.

"Come on, Luz. Do I have to? It feels silly to act like I'm proposing to you. There wasn't a set script I had." Putting my arms around his shoulders, I kissed him on the cheek and countered his argument.

"Cattaneo, I've seen you reenact entire *scenes* from *The Godfather*. How would this make you feel any less silly? I won't laugh, I promise." He let out an exasperated sigh as he got on his knees in front of me and kissed my fingers before he opened the box.

"This would have been a lot better at that fancy French restaurant." Taking his face in my hands, I pressed down on his cheeks begging him to take it seriously. He took another deep sigh but this time when he looked up at me, there was nothing but certainty in his eyes.

"Luz, since the day I met you, you've been my dream girl. To this day, it boggles my mind how two people who are so different, work so well together. Like an intricate puzzle, somehow, we just fit. It would be a fantasy made true if you would spend the rest of our lives putting the rest of the pieces together. Luz Marisol—"

"Yes," I blurted out cutting him off from his fake proposal. His thick brows furrowed in confusion.

"What?" he questioned, as I leaned in for a small peck on his lips.

"I said yes. I want to marry you." His bright eyes widened in surprise.

"You do?"

"Yes, silly. Will you put the ring on my finger already?" I demanded, but before I knew it he lifted me up in his arms and started bouncing me up and down, declaring that we were getting married in between kisses. If I had known he'd be this excited, I would have said yes the night he had planned to ask me.

"We have to tell your mom. *We have to tell my mom.* The whole world will pretty much know after that." He laid me back down on the bed as my eyes shot open to feel the stiffness of a hard on even his jeans couldn't hide.

"Boy, you are seriously hard right now?" His nose wrinkled, his wide green eyes reducing to slits.

"Um, excuse me. My girlfriend just became my fiancée. Forgive me for being a little excited." I gripped his length in my hands, a devious smile forming on my lips.

"Well, I mean, it'd be *foolish* to waste a perfectly good erection."

"Baby, you sure it's okay to fuck in your cousin's bed?" Was he really asking *me* that question?

"Correction. Guest bedroom. Besides, it's not like I'm not going to wash the sheets. Mikayla will be thrilled to find out we made up. She's not gonna mind us consummating our engagement." My lips met his in a light brush. "Now shut up and fuck me." His eyebrow cocked wetting his lips with a single swipe of his tongue.

"Okay, now you're actually sounding like a wife." He threw in with a roll of his eyes but wasted no time tracing a trail of kisses from my stomach to my thighs. There, his lips explored my hips and mound, tugging off my shorts and panties and heading straight for the place I so desperately needed him to be. His tongue teased me open with light playful licks that only intensified when I begged for more and with almost no effort, his strong arms gripped my thighs in a tight hold, using his fingers to reveal my clit.

"I fucking love eating your pussy," he confessed, as he dove back in to drive me to madness. It was one thing to sit back and enjoy the feel of his tongue on me, another to hear he loved tasting me. The sound of his sweet words were intoxicating, making me drunk with desire as he marked me as his.

"Don't stop, papi. Don't stop," I cried as my fingers tunneled through his soft hair. His mouth found my trigger and fired off short little licks and sucks making good on his promise not to stop.

"Evan, papi. I'm gonna come." My eyes closed shut as my legs clenched approaching a sweet release. "You gonna come from me, baby?" He asked in between his skillful mayhem and magic. Like a thief in the night, a soul shattering orgasm crashed my walls and robbed me of whatever sense I had left as I came painfully on his insatiable tongue.

"Damn, even I felt that one," Evan jested, stripping himself of his clothes as his hard length sprang free from the confinement of his jeans, a sigh escaping my lips blown away by my man's magnificence. I bit my lower lip as his weight settled on top of me but let out an unexpected cry when his thick hardness ripped through my entrance.

"What's wrong, baby? Too deep?" he asked with a raise of his eyebrows.

"Yeah, but maybe it's just the angle." I suggested, his hips adjusting and playing with positions until he found the right rhythm.

"Good?" His face a mask of strained pleasure at his slow controlled pace. My answer came with pulling his face close as I gave his lower lip a hungry nibble.

"I love you," I gasped, with each measured inch he plunged inside of me. The way his touch set fire to every part of my body, the lean hard beauty of his hips thrashing against me, even the way his breath whispered over my lips with each calculated stroke he rocked in to me. There wasn't a thing I *didn't* enjoy when Evan made love to me.

"Ah, fuck, Luz. I think I'm gonna come." He groaned, forcing me to wrap my legs around him to hold him captive to my lust. But it was no use, he spread my thighs and slammed into me rough and gasping until he let out a bone-deep growl of suppressed pleasure. He unleashed his love inside me, the hot spray of his seed racing at lightning speed, coating my core.

He leaned in to kiss my nose, catching his breath before pressing his sweaty forehead to mine. "You wear me out, woman. Fucking hell." Ignoring his sweat slicked body, I put my arms around his neck, pressing a light kiss to his lips.

"What are the chances of us going home early?" He leaned up swiping the sweat off his temple.

"Home early? Why?" he asked, as I laid a playful slap to his chest and dropped my lower lip because it was so obvious.

"Because, doofus, we have a wedding to plan."

CHAPTER NINETEEN

Evan

They say it's bad luck to see each other before the ceremony. For weeks both our moms tried to talk us out of having a first look, because in their eyes it wasn't traditional. It was bad enough we weren't getting married in a church but considering how nervous I was, I didn't mind getting up early ahead of time if it meant my nerves wouldn't show at the ceremony. The last thing I needed was a big bulk of Luz's family seeing me for the first time a nervous wreck. No, this was way better. Getting our wedding photos taken before took the pressure off and meant we would have more time for the reception and cocktail hour, something couples we talked to warned us about opting into, rather than to take their photos after the ceremony.

Luz wanted her hair and makeup to look fresh in the photos and personally, I just wanted her all to myself for a while. For us, it was a win-win. We had chosen the Brooklyn Botanical Garden because of its lush garden settings and outdoor options, and with Luz turning into the bridezilla I didn't know she had in her to be, she loved the glass-walled Palm House for the celebration afterwards. For someone so reluctant at first, she came around when all the planning took place but the second she got her dress, it was all she could talk about. I couldn't care less about a dress she would only be wearing for a good seven hours. I couldn't wait to get this over with because I missed the random Luz that brought up odd topics.

"Hey, just wanted to let you know she's finishing up now. Giving you an update in case you want to prep before we get started." Confused of what I should do, I probed the photographer, asking for suggestions and tips not to look awkward.

"Should I turn around or do I stay facing the door she's coming out of? Not really sure of the protocol." The photographer gave me this precious smile, like she knew I was nervous and patted me on the shoulder.

"There's really no wrong answer. But I do find it helpful when the groom waits until the bride's next to him to capture his first reaction. I don't care how many times you see your partner dressed up, that first time you see her in her wedding gown is a different kind of emotion. Just be natural and forget I'm here. When you see her, I'm sure it won't be hard to do." Taking a deep breath, I took her advice and faced the opposite direction. Admiring the lush green trees and myriad of colors blooming from nearby bushes, a tap to my shoulder reminded me that this was finally it. It was now or never.

The knots in my stomach seized as I turned around to face her. Her dress was strapless, long and ethereal with sheer billowy sleeves that started at the top of her arms and ended at her forearms. Small, matching white flowers adorned her curly updo in the fashion of a halo with soft makeup mimicking her typical beauty but enhanced it for a look that was damn near heavenly. The photographer was right. You could see your partner a million times dressed up, but nothing compared to a day like today. Fighting back tears, I covered my mouth, eyes wide at the sight in front of me. Luz smiled, reaching for my hands and taking them into hers.

"Will you please say something? You're making me nervous."

"Fuck, you look beautiful. Doesn't she look beautiful?" I asked our photographer, overlooking her advice to forget she was there as Luz played with the flaps of my tux jacket.

"You don't look so bad yourself, Cattaneo. This tux looks good on my future husband," she flirted, forcing me to pull her close and prepare for a smothering kiss.

"I mean it, you look really beautiful, Luz. I'm literally trying not to choke up with how breathtaking you look." I leaned in for another small kiss, nerves and anxiety easing up with every chance to kiss her lips.

"Oh my god, please stop. You're going to make me cry and my cousin is charging me industry rates for the day with no family discount," she joked. "The more I can be at one with my emotions, the less this is going to cost us."

"Look at you, finally worrying about the cost of everything. Listen, I promised you the wedding you deserve. You can afford to shed a few tears for your future *esposo*." The more we teased and talked, the easier it became to just focus on each other and block out the rest of the world. After posing for what felt like the one thousandth photo, the photographer's assistant came in to inform us that our bridal party had arrived as well as the family members we chose to be in the group photos.

"So it looks like everyone showed up early, which is great because I'm about to finish up here. I got some really great ones. You two are such a beautiful couple. You make super shooting super easy." Just as I planned to rush off, Luz pulled me behind a tall bush, concern swelling up in her lightly lined eyes.

"Quick confession. Our friends and family showing up makes it all real, and I'm nervous as hell. How can you look so at ease? Did you blaze up before we got here? Because I'm freaking out." Gripping her delicate shoulders, I helped steady her breathing to calm her nerves.

"Baby, freaking out is okay. Just don't go acting on fear and have me stranded at the altar," I joked. She shook her head as her dangly earrings moved with her.

"Trust me, my whole family is here. I'm not going nowhere. My mini sprite for a mom would probably bring me back kicking and screaming. Besides, if I don't go through with it, that lifetime promise of homemade cannolis goes right out the window. And you know how much I love cannolis. Especially yours," she teased, getting that last laugh in before we reunited with our families. Switching back to being serious, I asked if she had any last words as my girlfriend, seeing as the next time we saw each other after the photos we would no longer be engaged.

"Yeah, just one thing actually. Thanks for being so trash at math. We might not have made it this far if you were actually passing calc senior year," she said with an attempt to run off but with my need to get the last word, I pulled her right back.

"Okay, first off wasn't failing calc, I just needed *tutoring*. Either way, I'm glad it was you. I was already obsessed with you. The tutor sessions just gave me an in." I gave her one last hug before suggesting we regroup for the photos.

"Now let's hurry up and take these photos so we can be married already."

***

For a brief period, time stood still. I should have been paying more attention to the cleric's sermon about the two found souls destined to find each another. Instead all I could focus on was how stunning Luz looked and how nothing else mattered in this moment.

"And now the rings" she said, knocking me out of my stupor to concentrate on the task at hand.

"Now before we recite the final vows, your fiancée spoke with me earlier about reading her own," she admitted, taking me by surprise considering she hadn't told me before today she was writing her own. Everything I wanted to say to her, I told her every day, but given we were in a space with two hundred plus of our family members and friends, a quick heads up would have been nice.

"I'm sorry, Evan. It was so last minute. I promise I wasn't trying to outdo you or anything. It's just you know, I'm a writer. This shouldn't surprise you." Being her usual brazen self, she turned to our guests explaining how bad she was at memorizing things and how not to laugh at her hiding place because she had to put it *somewhere*. From her bosom, she pulled out a folded piece of colored paper as the guests roared in laughter at her cheeky display. I couldn't do anything but laugh along with them because, I mean, none of this surprised me about her. If anyone could make a serious moment funny, it was Luz. Turning to our friends and family, I gestured toward her adding to everyone's joy and entertainment.

"You see what I have to deal with? I can't take this one anywhere." Our guests calmed down long enough to give Luz a chance to clear her throat and read her vows.

"Evan Giovanni Cattaneo. The boy who worked my last nerve to charm his way into my heart. In this lifetime, I've been fortunate enough to fall in love before you, and even more fortunate to fall in love twice after our first run ended. They haven't always been healthy. They haven't always been fulfilling. And that's where your love felt different. You've always loved me openly and proudly. Often times when I didn't even deserve it. When the right person loves you, the wall you spend years building after someone hurts you comes down only to reveal a gentler, selfless, more considerate version of yourself. That's what your love did for me. I'm not always the easiest to love, but I never know it with a caring, thoughtful and giving man like you. I may not ever live up to your expectations, but I hope I can spend a lifetime proving myself wrong." This time I didn't even try fighting back the tears. Things got so intense to where my dad actually stood up and encouraged me to get it all out. Before I knew it, everyone stood up clapping and yelled encouraging words that helped me pull myself together long enough and continue on with the ceremony.

"With this ring," we repeated after the cleric, moments after exchanging our bands.

"For better or for worse." Shit getting realer with each repeated passage.

"Do you, Luz, take Evan, to be your lawfully wedded husband?"

With a smile that showed both rows of her teeth she is enthusiastically stated, "I do."

"And do you, Evan, take Luz to be your lawfully wedded wife?"

"I do," I said before she could get the last word out.

In a montage of pretty words, we were announced husband and wife, a flood of emotions compelling me to pick her up and spin her around and plant a kiss that was full of tongue like we were in private. No one on our guest list needed to get that up close and personal with us, but this was our wedding day, everyone was just going to have to be understanding.

For the first dance, Luz had changed into something shorter and sultrier, a flesh toned dress that blended in with her shade of brown and hugged her curves in *all* the ways. While I've never been much of a dancer, they decided on a song that made it impossible not to find the rhythm in and after a while, I just zoned the room out and put my focus on her.

"You know you in this dress just further confirms I have the sexiest wife in the world. It's easy to picture you naked when you wear this flesh tone stuff."

"Yeah, well as beautiful as that wedding dress was, lugging around that train wasn't the funnest thing in the world. But this dress we can totally sneak away for a quickie without even taking it off," she joked. As tempted as I was to take her up on that offer, we had a late-night flight to catch to a place in paradise where we could do all the screwing we wanted. For now, I just wanted to celebrate with our families while we still had the venue. The dance floor swelled with people only moments after the first dance concluded, and the liquor finally hitting everyone's systems caused the DJ to transition to a more upbeat song.

"What your dad said over the toast was sweet. I'm a Cattaneo now." She mimicked my dad's thick Bronx accent. "I didn't know how much I needed to hear someone call me the daughter they never had. Sometimes I wish I still had my dad around, but I love that your family fully embraced me," she said as I wiped a tear from her eye. For now, Luz would be a Cattaneo in spirit only, something I was fine with. We discussed changing her surname beforehand and because hers was a link to her cultural identity and a way she honored her father, we both agreed she'd only change it once we started having kids. I was wise enough to realize that marriage was so much more than last names, and compromising was the only thing that brought us this far.

"Hey, you never told me where we were going on our honeymoon," she scolded with a light slap to my chest.

"Because the whole concept of being a surprise is that it stays a surprise. You've been asking me for weeks now. Don't worry, I know you'll love it."

"Evan, I'm not getting on a plane without knowing what kind of hair products I'm going to need to combat the environment."

I voiced my frustration with a theatrical groan, rolling my eyes at Luz always managing to get her way. Definitely the downside to spoiling her.

"Okay, fine. We're going to Seychelles." With a flash wave of excitement, Luz screamed, bouncing up and down on her heels before leaning in to bless me with another kiss. For ten days it would be nothing but rest and relaxation and a distraction from our lives back home. We were already making a checklist of all the new toys and the sexual acts we planned to take part in. We pinky swore not to leave the island until we checked everything on the list, so the earlier we checked in, hell, the earlier we could start.

At last, the afternoon for us had come to an end. We literally only had hours to get out of these clothes and catch our late-night flight so the thanks-for-joining-us's and so-happy-you-could-make-it's came out in hurried exchanges.

"Lucy, I know you're not going to just leave without throwing the bouquet. Come on. It's tradition," her aunt Zahira demanded. Luz and I decided to skip the whole garter toss game since it made me uncomfortable at the thought of people fighting over something I pulled off my wife's leg. She wanted to keep her bouquet, but after nudging her that we were short on time, we both agreed that it would die anyway. Why not just let the woman have their little fun?

Turning to me, she tossed it behind her to a sea full of female family members, as it landed unexpectedly in the hands of the youngest adult woman in attendance, Luz's baby cousin Demeter. Her face soured, proving that a relationship, let alone a marriage, was probably the last thought on her mind. Luz and I laughed as she tried to pass it off to one of Luz's friends but every last one of them declined leaving her stuck with it, as we said our final goodbyes.

EPILOGUE

Evan

"Luz, this better be the last photo because I'm getting tired," I said, taking what felt like the millionth photo I snapped of her surrounded in an army of cane corso/rottweiler mix puppies. She was getting carried away with their IG page content, something she spent all month building and curating without any input from me. Bringing an adorable puppy to her face, it covered her in dog licks and kisses.

"Just one more. I want a lot to choose from because last time I looked busted in all the photos and only used the ones I wasn't in. Their new posts have to be up by the end of the day, or their followers are going to have a fit!" I shook my head in disbelief. Did she even hear herself? I'll admit Luz was pretty good at the social media stuff. Melo and Mary's couple page had surpassed even her fifty thousand followers, and if you had told me that people would be interested in following two dogs in love, I would have laughed you out of Manhattan. But once Miss Mary Mack pushed out those babies, the Melo and Mary love just kept growing. As much as it was a pain to get Mary back in hot dog summer shape due to her age and the weight she gained to carry five puppies, she was finally back to her energetic, destructive self. Something we learned early she'd already passed down to her pups.

"Are they to your liking?" I handed her my phone before sprawling on the couch nearby. Miss Mary Mack jumped on top of me and made herself comfortable across my lap, while Melo sat lazily on his dog bed, observing. The only one unphased from all the energy they required was Luz. It was all kinds of adorable.

"Woooo... Thumper, you need a bath like ASAP! I'm guessing you're the one who left that little surprise for me in my favorite flats." I sat up to see her petting him but after a few weeks of wondering how Luz distinguished them all, I wondered why she even bothered since for now we only had the room and time for just two besides Carmelo and Miss Mary Mack. The rest were promised to interested and eager pet owners.

"Baby, remind me which one is Thumper again?" Knowing it would push her buttons to ask but never failing to get entertainment out of it while I still could.

"Urgh! Evan, you do this every time," she berated as I tried my hardest to fight back laughter.

"You have to be better at telling them apart. You are not leaving that spot until you get it right. See it as practice because what if we have twins one day. You have to be more proactive about learning their differences." Did she just compare human twins to dog twins? That was *completely* different. With people I'd have voices and human personalities to work with. Every parent knew how to tell their own human children apart. Talk about unhealthy attachments. I sat up ignoring her whole speech about how maybe if I spent more time with them, I wouldn't have this problem and took a lazy guess.

"That's Thumper. He's the real hyper one. The one that's always getting into trouble." I said and pointed. That one was a little easier since he had this little brown spot by his nose. I rolled the dice and took another guess. "Beetlejuice." Luz's eyes flashed open in disbelief.

"No. That's Pray-tell. You know the bougie one, that's picky about what she's eats and is always throwing shade. *This* is Beetlejuice." She lifted him up in her arms and kissed him on the nose, proving that they looked the exact same. I rested my chin in my hands.

"Right, right, right. Because he's the one always making the funny faces and only comes to you after you call him three times. Shit, I thought I had that one." I pointed to another cutie positive I'd get the last two considering it was a fifty percent chance I'd get it right. "That one is Iroh. The one that tore through all my Moroccan mint tea bags I waited for three months for Trader Joe's to restock," I hissed, only to have Luz make excuses for her.

"She can't help herself. She loves her tea." Loves her tea, my ass. That only left the last pup Michele. I wasn't so bad at this. Luz's face lit up with a wide smile as she clapped her hands to congratulate me. As fun as it was playing the guessing game, I was relieved we'd already decided that we were just keeping Pray Tell and Michele. Iroh and Thumper, I predicted, would be the wild tag team that outdid Melo and Mary combined, and Beetlejuice? Let's just say letting Luz name them all was going to leave me tongue tied and flustered saying that three times fast. The only issue was she was already getting attached to them like we were keeping them all and I knew we were going to have our hands full with four fully grown dogs. I didn't even want to think about it.

For an entertaining five minutes, Luz crawled around like a toddler, followed by a mob of five puppies as they made their way to the kitchen squealing and barking in unmeasured enjoyment. When Luz stood up, I centered my gaze back on Melo who was now cozied up with Mary unaffected by the noise from the other room. Awww...

"Hey, is this mail from the other day?" she questioned, flipping through some letters on the counter and ripping a few open like it was a check. I shrugged. Who really opened bills anymore?

"I don't know, babe. I didn't look." I turned back in her direction to witness her jumping up and down like she had won something, but before I could ask her what it was, she ran over and handed it to me, begging me to read it myself.

"This letter officiates your legal name change from Luz Marisol De los Santos to Luz Marisol Cattaneo." I read the last line in confusion. We'd only been married a few months, and I respected her keeping her last name. I hoped she didn't do it for me. "Okay, I'm confused. You know I respected you keeping your last name until we—" Before I could finish the sentence, she rolled her eyes in a playful way, rubbing her stomach forcing me off the couch.

"What are you telling me?" Knowing the answer, but refusing to believe it until she said the words.

"I'm telling you...that pretty soon I won't be as good at hiding it like Miss Mary Mack was." My eyes widened in shock as I raked my fingers through my hair.

"Holy shit. We have to take a pregnancy test." I grabbed her wrist in excitement as she fought me to stay in one spot.

"Evan, cool it. When my period didn't come on time, I took one the other day. And just to make sure I wasn't freaking out, I went and saw my doctor and she confirmed what the test said. Obviously, I'm not the preferred age most women get pregnant. But she assured me even at thirty-four, I could have a safe and successful pregnancy. You are now looking at the host of what I believe will be the dopest small human to ever live." Words were leaving her mouth but all I could manage to piece together was that she had known for days what I was just discovering. I cannot be held accountable for my next words and actions. I was going to be a father.

"Luz, I don't care what your doctor said. I want to take a pregnancy test. I want to see the positive results for myself," I said, slapping on a baseball cap and slipping on my socks and shoes, wondering why she wasn't doing the same.

"I waited two years for us to get this excited over you peeing on a stick. You're not about to take that away from me." She crossed her arms, her eyes widening incredulously.

"Boy, I don't even have to pee."

"*Welp*, you should have thought about that. Put your coat on, it's going to take us ten minutes to walk to Duane Reade. You might as well grab a water and start loading up before we get back." Luz stomped her bare feet with her fists close to her sides.

"You're sapping all the fun out of what I thought would be good news." You know what? She was right, I was overreacting and had to calm down. Aside from the barking puppies, we stared at each other with loss for words until I broke the silence.

"Fuck. We're going to become parents." I took Luz into my arms, spinning her around until she complained of dizziness. When did women start experiencing morning sickness? Was I only making it worse? I needed to call my mother. I had to tell my family.

"Well, I'm glad you're excited," she finally said, naive to the actual reason I was overcome with joy.

"Luz, baby, I wish it were that simple. It just dawned on me that everything you said you *wouldn't* do, you caved for little ole me. I got you to remarry. You changed your last name, and now there's a little us growing inside of you. If I didn't know any better, I think you might actually be in love with me." She flashed me the signature scowl she reserved for when I got on her nerves. This was the one moment it felt like it was worth it.

"Evan, you never fail to make what could have been a heartfelt moment weird. *But* to entertain your declaration, yes, I broke all my rules for...you. Congratulations, Cattaneo. You turned a Luz into a housewife," she teased. Pulling her in close, I pressed a deep kiss to her full lips.

"No. I turned a Luz into *my* wife." Leaning back into meet her lips for another kiss. Luz was untraditional in *all* ways wife material, but that was what I loved about her. I wouldn't have traded her for anyone else in the world. Our kiss was interrupted by three out of five puppies clawing at our pant legs begging for our attention. When Mary stepped in, fully rested from her nap, she took one of the little pups by the neck with her teeth and scooped another behind her leg at an attempt to give us some privacy.

"Awwww...look how comfortable Mary falls into the role of being a nagging mother. That's going to be you someday." I fake cried, her push shoving me onto the couch as her words scolded me in Spanish. Not long after she laid down on top of me, relieving me of my baseball cap and tossing it across the room closer to my collection.

"I'm really happy," she added with a warm smile.

"Me too, baby," I said leaning in for yet another kiss. I was definitely in the mood for what resulted from our constant kissing and for a good nine months, I didn't have to worry about pulling out or pharmacy trips for Plan B. My sexy momma to be was already carrying, which reminded me...

"Just one more thing since you seem to have a unique approach to name giving. Massimo's not even a consideration. And don't try to convince me because it's completely off the table. *However*, I am open to Italian names..."

EXTENDED EPILOGUE

Evan

After an hour of tummy time, I was ecstatic to have finally tired the little one out. After four months, we were proud to say we were sleeping a whole six hours and not walking around looking like the walking dead. Luke was growing bigger and more curious with everything. He'd inherited a blend of light brown skin unique to dual heritage, but his expressive green eyes were all Cattaneo. The more I spent time with him, the more I could see Luz's personality sprouting from his sixteen week old smile. He was so damn cute, cuter than I ever was as a baby. Sometimes it was hard to believe you were a part of making small versions of yourselves.

"All right, buddy, let's get you ready for bed before Mami gets back." Walking him over to the crib that slept a few feet away from our bed. Because things had happened so fast we hadn't gotten around to moving into a bigger place, but the plan was once Luke was old enough to where we didn't worry about him sleeping in another room by himself, we would buy a house in the suburbs.

There were already a few places outside the city we were

considering but nothing definite until we are serious about it. As much as we both love the city, it wasn't where we wanted to raise our future family and truthfully, I wanted something for us that felt like ours from the start. Luz had done her best shifting things around, but I couldn't wait for her to have her own walk in-closet. Heaven knows she needed it with how all my suits were suffering from the lack of space.

Out of nowhere Luz materialized at the nearby wardrobe wearing a knee length satin robe, her face free of makeup and her curly hair big and untamed. From the dresser she pulled out a pair of panties and slipped into them just as I'd finished securing Luke's swaddle. "I don't know what's been with Luciano today. It took him forever to get tired. I was doing our little dances. Read him a few new stories with all my funny voices he likes. I just hope he sleeps all night like he did the other day. A guy could get used to getting a full night's rest." I made my way over to the foot of our bed sitting down and leaning on my elbows to watch Luz finish up her skin care routine, rolling a roller over her clean skin.

"I feel like you set the standard too high with your version of story time. Now, he always cries whenever I try to read to him. I know he's only four months but he has to understand Mami too tired to distinguish all those damn voices, so you're going to get this story read the text to speech version." I didn't blame her. For fifteen weeks she had been the person Luke saw for most of the day, one of the many reasons I rushed home to give her the afternoon to herself. Now that she was back at the job, I was sure work was a little break from being at home all day. We both have our strengths and weaknesses and my strength was reigning supreme at story time.

"I see someone got their nails done. End of your first week, are we glad to be back?"

She had been on paid maternity leave for twelve weeks and decided to take her bosses' offer to work from home. And *that* lasted a total of three weeks after discovering it was hard to attend to a baby and meet her office commitments. In the meantime, her aunt Noelia had offered to watch him in the mornings because she loved babies, and it gave her someone to take care of while both her adult children were out of the house. Surprisingly enough, Luz and her aunt's relationship had drastically improved from all the horror stories she never failed to share. Gone was the bitter judgmental auntie and here was the sweet third grandmother. I think she just missed having her kids around, and having that help while Luz and I worked was a godsend as we regained some normalcy balancing the adjustments it took becoming first time parents.

"Ehhh...it's all right, I guess. I just feel like so much has changed since I've been gone. They pretty much remodeled the entire office and there are all these new interns now. Not even including these new inside jokes without me. And get this, Gen has a new work husband. Like damn, I haven't even been gone that long." Oblivious to who she was talking about, I racked my brain trying to remember who that was.

"Gen's the short one right? The one you went to pride with last year and who got us the Snoo crib?" Luz had so many friends. Far more that she kept in touch with than I did. But Candice was the only one I saw all the time so unless I gave them a nickname to help me remember them, I found myself lost in her hilarious work gossip. "Yeah," she said with a cute pout of her lips. "The hoe had me thinking I was irreplaceable."

Sitting up, I reached for her hand and pulled her closer to me. There was a certain reluctance with her enthusiasm, but I just chalked it up to her having a less than stellar week. That and ever since she had the baby she was so protective of her body. Almost like she didn't want me to touch her, but I knew if I let her crawl her way into a hole of self-consciousness, it would take her forever to get her to see what I saw.

"Well, it's a good thing your *real* husband thinks you're invaluable. I would never for a second think about replacing you. How about...we spend...the next hour or so...reminding you why?" It wasn't hard to notice Luz's sex drive had taken a hit the second she had given birth to our son. It had been months and that wasn't like Luz at all. We both had our hands full with how taxing it was caring for a newborn. But what we both needed was some quality time together something that didn't include changing diapers or drawing straws to which one of us was going to tend to his cries.

"The doctor said it was okay after eight weeks. To be honest, I figured you'd be mauling me by now, considering you asked the obstetrician a million questions." Tousling the loose stray curls around her eyes, she relaxed in my embrace and caressed the nape of my neck.

"Yeah, well, I haven't been feeling like myself lately. It's like I'm proud of what my body is capable of. I hosted a whole ass little human minute. But I don't know, I look in the mirror and I don't recognize my body anymore. I'm all lumpy in places I'm not used to carrying weight in, and as far as my breasts go, Luke is taking everything and just leaving me the saggy scraps. I just haven't been feeling that sexy." She confirmed what I already assumed, now it was my job to convince her otherwise.

"Luz, I am in awe of you. The amount of vulnerability and humility you've shown me in these past thirteen months has been life changing. For nine months you carried our baby and for four you've been so patient with me while you catch me up to speed on the things that come naturally for you becoming a mother. You're a goddess in my eyes, and I just want to worship you. At least let me help you forget with my head between your legs." At that she rolled her eyes, her two tone lips forming an expression of disbelief.

"That's easy for you to say. Nothing about your appearance has changed. You're still all hard and well maintained. You don't even have any bald spots or gray hair yet. That shit isn't even fair," she joked, but I knew it was her way of deflecting how she really felt about her body changing, something that didn't cross my mind at all.

"That's because I always want to look good for you." It wasn't like I could help that I had all my hair and hadn't had any grays sprouting as of yet, but if it made her feel better, I was finally feeling the effects of coaching youth basketball trying to keep up with their teenage endurances. Didn't exactly deter me away from tiring myself through fucking. Most men always made time for that, even in pain. With layers between us, I planted a few kisses on her stomach, my palm caressing the inside of her thighs, just to have her jerk away from me.

"I know we haven't had much of a chance to be close in a while, but I can't help feeling like you feel like I don't desire you. You're always rushing to cover up and you don't think I noticed but I do. Every time. If you don't come out of the bathroom fully clothed, you put on your panties and bra with your clothes already on. I just want you to feel good about yourself like you always do." Pulling her back to me my lips met her stomach again in a closed mouth kiss.

"I'd feel more confident if I could keep my shirt on." Now that gave me pause. What, were we seventeen again?

"*Argh*! Luz, I would rather jerk off in the shower than to fuck you with your clothes on. If it's not all of you, skin the skin, then I'll just wait until you're more ready."

"Evan, I'm trying to compromise," she argued but for someone who had gone weeks without masturbating, I knew I can go another sixteen weeks before I agreed to *that*.

"Just let me make you feel good. I promise not to wake the baby. And if he wakes up, I'll take him to the recliner and let you get some rest tonight. Hell, I'll even let you sleep in and cook you breakfast. Reintroduce my back to that new manicure of yours."

"*Boy*, you do that every Saturday anyways." She pointed a finger between the center of my eyes and pushed my head back coaxing a smile out of me.

"Yeah, but this time you'd sleep amazing because you got fucked. Even you can't deny there's no sleep like put you to sleep fucking. Plus, I got you something." Her skeptical left brow lifted as she made the quick walk to her nightstand to take the gift in question out of the top drawer.

"Is it a cock ring?" She held it up in her hands, bewildered by its design easing my own initial confusion. If I appreciated anything about our sex life, it was that Luz loved her toys.

"The woman at the shop had nothing but nice things to say about it and these little things right here are for your clit...I think," I said turning my head, hoping it felt better than it looked. This was her expertise and I was the one who just figured things out by trying.

"I feel like this will be loud and I don't want to wake Luke up," she stressed, defeated and tired. I couldn't exactly blame her because at this stage he was such a light sleeper.

Grabbing the baby monitor in one hand and leading Luz into the living room, I relaxed my arms around her, the sweet smell of her hair having a revitalizing effect on my mood. "But what if he wakes up?"

"Then we'll hear it."

"But what if he started crying?"

"We're just a few rooms away."

"But what if..." Pressing my finger to her lips, I silenced her pessimistic protests.

"Enough with the buts. Unless it's yours and I'm slapping it," I teased, making her laugh and mark my chest in a playful smack. Whatever was in our hands we laid on the coffee table re-familiarizing our lips in a long brazen kiss that held nothing back. "Mmmm...I just want to taste you," I whispered leaving behind a trail of kisses along her neck line, shoulders and whimpering throat.

"*Ahem*. I just want to warn you that the housekeeping is not to my usual standards." Easing her robe off her body, I tried to make it perfectly clear with my eyes and words that there was nothing she could say to turn me off right now. "Yeah, that's literally never stopped me before."

"I know, it's just I feel like it's gonna show if I'm insecure with how long it takes me to climax."

"Shhh...not another word. Just lie back and get comfortable," I requested with the only acceptable reason for her to get up was if wanted to tie her hair up. A wild haired Luz wasn't a happy Luz, so imagine my surprise when she said it could wait. I kissed her stomach through her sleep shirt while my hands caressed her fuller thighs and edge of her panties. Letting a curious finger find a way inside, I was pleased to know that while she wasn't waxed, she was trim, which was my preference over bare any day of the week. "All these clothes," I said frustrated helping her out of her sleep shirt revealing a flesh toned nursing bra and underwear I wasn't used to seeing her in considering how high it went up to cover her stomach. As I lowered down to kiss her neck and shoulders I unclasped her bra only to be met with a brief warning.

"So because I haven't pumped all day, there's probably going to be some leakage. My nipples are going through it right now, so can you be delicate?" I nodded my lips sucking her nipple with a ravenous gentleness.

"Like that?"

"Mmmmm...just like that." She ended in a soft moan as her eyes fluttered shut. She laid back, my body blanketing her as I alternated her other breast between my lips, thankful that something so small made her feel so good. She did leak a little but it wasn't weird or odd tasting. It was actually kind of sweet and a strangely surprise after months of not being intimate. The way she relaxed under my mouth assured me she was ready for more and I was ready to give it to her.

Inch by inch, I kissed down to her stomach, her panties coming off with a drastic tug. There wasn't a spot on her body my lips neglected as I kissed from her ankles to her soft brown thighs, her sweet whimpers causing all the blood in my veins to rush to my cock. Now aroused,

she drew herself closer to me begging, almost crying for me to taste her. Raking her fingers through my hair my tongue explored her soft at first, intensity rising when she eased into it and melded into my embrace. I for one was starving for her, a famished animal that had been deprived of his favorite prey for months as I licked my feast clean. My cock grew harder as she squirmed underneath me, her legs tightening around my willing neck.

"Oh, Papi, I'm gonna come," she said looking at me helplessly through lust filled eyes. If it wasn't for her tells, I would have questioned how quickly she was able to reach her peak, but her reaction couldn't lie. Her body shuddered, conceding to her sweet release. Licking any remains of her orgasm clean, I nuzzled against the inside of her thighs gauging her reaction to see if she wanted to go further.

"Someone looks like they're having fun." Making my way up her body, she wrapped her arms around my neck and planted an affection kiss against my lips. I still tasted like her. I wasn't in a rush to wipe her away in case it took another sixteen weeks for us to make love again.

"I feel like I want to keep going, but I'm terrified it's gonna hurt. When I was home all day with nothing but time to myself, I read all these horror stories about how everything feels down there. What if I hate sex after this?"

"Well, if it hurts we'll stop, okay? If you're nervous, we don't even have to go that far. We can test things how things feel for you with my fingers, and if you can't handle it, we can try for another time." With Luz in agreement, I covered my fingers in the nearby lube and almost stopped when she winced at my fingers meeting her opening. "You okay baby?" She took a deep breath trying to relax but settled on asking me to sit beside her and distracting her with kissing. She moaned, losing herself in the moment with each passing kiss as her fear eased up, allowing me to plunge deeper until I found that spot that drove her crazy. Fingers deep inside her, it wasn't long before she wanted more and happily straddled me as she reached for the cock ring on the coffee table beside us.

"Wait, you think we should strap up? Can't you still get pregnant again this soon after? I want another baby but not *that* damn soon." Placing the toy at the base of my cock she flicked the on switch as the unexpected vibration caused me to flinch out of shock.

"It's cool. I'll just get the morning after pill in the morning. No big deal," she announced before slowly sinking onto my cock, all tension and thoughts dissolving in one fluid motion.

"Fuck, I missed this pussy," I said within an attempt to grip her hips, only to have her pin my hands to each side of the couch.

"No, let me do it. You might be too rough. If I can control the depth and pace you won't have to worry about hurting me."

"If you wanted to fuck me, next time say less," I teased, reaching into kiss her. Hot, slick and ready to grip every inch, she rode my cock, slowly at first until she gathered her rhythm and confidence to do more. With wild recklessness, it appeared Luz was back to her old self, riding me carelessly in a way that sent us straight to the floor, my ass taking the brunt of the fall. It was more funny than it was painful and it was nice to take the seriousness away long enough to laugh it off and get back to the task at hand.

"Damn, I'm sorry. That clit motion was feeling *too* good. I just got lost in the moment," she joked. "But I'm think I'm ready for some mutual thrusting considering I almost rode your dick off."

"No, I think you just like it when I fuck you. Which lucky for you, I like doing most of the work. Your little bull riding act has me hard as fuck."

"Oh, just shut up and fuck me," she demanded, forcing me to take hold of her waist and piston my hard length into her. Wrapping her arms around my neck, her moans and cries for me to fuck her hard abandoned any promise we made to keep quiet as sweat lined our bodies with every thrust.

"You like that cock deep inside you baby?" I asked, knowing I was close but holding off until I knew where she was. The last thing I needed was to end things before she had enough time to climax. Through gritted teeth, she confessed how much she loved my big cock and how good it felt for me to be inside her. Asking her to come...*no* telling her to, was a surefire way to get her there. She was far from submissive but nothing made her wet like barking a command.

"You want to come on his cock, baby? I want to fill you up with come but first, you're gonna come on this dick."

"I love it when you tell me to." Her breath a hot caress against my skin. By now we were both hot sweaty messes, her usually defined curls a thick mass of frizz and dishevelment and yet, she'd never looked more beautiful.

"Mmmmm..." With a slap of her ass and a pull to her hair, I pressed my lips to her salty neck and watched as she writhed at my command. "Come on this fucking cock."

In a mutual struggle of met thrusts, her body went taut, succumbing to pleasure's prison before she could warn me of her climax. The fury of my deep thrusts filled her until finally, I surrendered to her tight warmth, coming inside her with the strength of a storm. It had only been four months but damn, it felt like it had been twice that, a year even. If she wasn't up at eight am to get that morning after pill, I sure as hell would beat her to it. Not waiting a second for me to catch my breath, Luz leaned in and kissed me, wiping the hair plastered to my forehead away with her newly manicured nails.

"Luz, I'm always gonna have the hots for you. Don't you fuckin' dare make me wait that long unless medically necessary," I said before leaning in for another sweaty kiss, only to sigh in frustration when Luke's cries through the baby monitor took me out of the moment.

"Shit." Luz sighed, matching my frustration as she pressed her clammy body into me and wrapped her arms around the base of my neck.

"You sure you want another one of those?" Adjusting her so she could see my sincerity, with the palm of my hand I brushed a portion of her thick hair out of her eyes.

"As long as it's with you, without a doubt in my mind."

The End

Did you read this book out of sequence?

If you have, don't forget to read The Love Bet, book one in the Love Unexpected series!

Thanks so much for making it all the way to the end of Luz and Evan's story!

We so hope you devoured it! Before you go, we'd love if you could leave a few short words of what you thought of The Engagement Plan!

Follow this link to review and tell others what you thought. Again, thank you for your purchase and be sure to flip through the end pages to discover more addictive reads from G.L. Tomas.

Don't forget to pre-order The Hook-Up Games, book three in the Love Unexpected series!

And Vinh and Mikayla's unlikely match story continues in book 1 of the Flirty Kinkster App series, Click to Subscribe releasing later this year!

Happy Reading!

PLEASE CONSIDER REVIEWING THE ENGAGEMENT PLAN!

Will you consider helping us grow as authors?

Did you like/love this book? Would you like to see more from this series?

Please consider leaving a review! We knew as a reader you're beat over the head with *please leave a review*, but reviews are one of the many parts that aid in a book's visibility but also guide an author into knowing what their audience wants.

Maybe we have another story cooking up! But we may not prioritize it if we're not sure the world wants it!

Reviews help us cater to the reader and center on the series' an author wants to finish but isn't sure due to the radio silence. So before you flip past this page, consider reviewing this title. We'll even make it easier for you!

Click here to review this book!

Spare one square for your possibly new favorite author!

If you'd like more updates from us but don't like emails, consider joining our exclusive Facebook Group!

AVAILABLE FOR PRE-ORDER: THE HOOK-UP GAMES

Twelve weeks in the tropics where ten sexy singles battle over a twisted game of temptation. For two contestants, one careless one nightstand changed all the rules...

Content creator Demeter Singh has a lifelong dream of becoming a celebrity makeup artist. Wouldn't hurt if she were able to open up her own beauty bar on the way there.

Her business plan? Solid!

Her vision? Airtight!

Now she just needed the money to *finance* it. After being turned down by her family for help, she takes matters into her own hands.

Signing up to compete on the world's new biggest dating show ***The Hook-Up Games*** was not in her manifestations but with a grand prize of ***150k***, she'll do anything to fight her way to the end. Even if it means resisting her unforgettable one-night stand...

Fitness influencer Loren Gagnon is the boy your parents warned you about. ***Tattooed***. Slick-talking and a smile that brings good girls to their knees. He didn't fall hard easily but when Demeter disappeared without even a name after a passionate late night romp, he's been determined to win her over even if it means going home without a cash prize.

The rules for the hook-up games are simple.

No kissing

No sucking

No f*cking

Shouldn't be so hard, right?

The Hook Up Games is a full length AMBW new adult romance with a sexy Chinese-Québécois hero and a heroine who fights her hardest to deny the mutual attraction.

Available Now for Pre-Order

AVAILABLE FOR PRE-ORDER: CLICK TO SUBSCRIBE

Meet Vinh Nguyen.

Daddy Dominant. PhD. And now host of the new online relationship advice show, The Dating Deal.

Things in his life were going according to plan until his dream match on Flirty Kinkster ghosted him after a lust-filled night of bliss. Little does he know, the show's producers secured a co-host to offer a *woman's* perspective.

Mikayla Morales, the oh-so-tempting Dating Coach is everything he isn't. Anti-relationship. Type A. And most importantly, no man's submissive.

When the producers pitch the idea of them faking a relationship for ratings, Mikayla finds herself feeding into an attraction she thought she wanted no part in. So why is the fantasy becoming everything she could only dream of?

Vinh's determined to convince his dream girl, when it comes to love, he's just the man for the job. **Because once you spend one night with Daddy, you'll always wanna play...**

Pre-order here

Click To Subscribe is a spicy single dad romance with no cheating and a guaranteed HEA. It features a fake relationship that becomes oh-so-real, spicy bedroom times and just a lil' bit of spanking. It is for mature audiences, so if amazing bedroom scenes aren't your thing, sit this one out. But if you like a little kink, this is the read for you.

AVAILABLE NOW: THE LOVE BET

Magazine journalist Luz knows plenty about sex and hookups — after all, that's her specialty. But when she's assigned to write a column for Valentine's Day, she decides to use the opportunity to answer a question: Will three nights of mind-blowing sex cause a person to fall in love? Luz doubts it, but her former flame Evan is ready to take on the challenge…

Available Now(also in Audio!)

ALSO BY G.L. TOMAS

Love Unexpected Series:

Love finds even those not looking!

The Love Bet (Also available in audio)

The Engagement Plan

The Hook-Up Games (Available for Pre-order)

Kinky Matchmaker Series:

Kinksters find their perfect naughty match!

Made For You (Available for Pre-order)

Meant For You (Also available in audio)

Melt For You (Also available in audio)

More For You(sign up to learn when it drops)

Friends That Have Sex Series:

A love pessimist and gentle bad boy can't get enough of each other...

F*THS (Also available in audio)

Friends That Still... (Also available in audio)

Friends That Break (Available for pre-order)

Friends That Collide (Available for pre-order)

Bookish Friends To Lovers Series:

Book lovers find they have more than enough in common to take it there despite the circumstances.

Same Page (Also available in audio)

Next Chapter (Also available in audio)

Pagebreak (Available for pre-order)

Bookmark (sign up to learn when it drops)

Flirty Kinkster App Series:

Click To Subscribe (Available now for pre-order)

Standalones:

But I'm Not a Robot (Also available in audio)

Lucky's Charm

ACKNOWLEDGMENTS

Magnolia Author Services, you helped us in a pinch! A big thanks to Najla Qamber for helping us with such amazing branding! Also, a huge thanks/hugs for everyone who pre-ordered The Engagement Plan! You helped us push through!

ABOUT THE AUTHOR

G.L. Tomas is a twin writing duo and lover of all things blerdy, fearless and fun. When they're not spending their time crafting swoon-worthy heroes, they're battling alien forces in other worlds but occasionally take days off in search mom and pop spots that make amazing pasteles and tostones fried to perfection.

They host salsa lessons and book boyfriend auditions in their secret headquarters located in Connecticut.

Head over to our Official website @ GLTomaswrites.com There we have a list of our upcoming titles and you can purchase our paperbacks directly, along with other swag!

Jump on over to our official The Love Bet Pinterest board to see our fantasy casts and dream-ups of the characters!

Sign up for G.L. Tomas' newsletter.

You'll get exclusives, such as book release updates, chances to win or earn free swag, access to well thought-out book lists, and opportunities to save on books before anyone else!

Don't forget to connect with us on Bookbub and our exclusive Facebook Group! And be sure to send us an email to talk books and about your fave characters! Drop us a line at guinevere.libertad@gltomaswrites.com

We're now on TikTok! If you love book recs, be sure to follow us!

If you liked reading The Engagement Plan as much as we did writing it, please consider leaving a review! Reviews are a huge part of how other readers discover and judge a book. It may seem like such a small gesture but it's a small gesture that goes a long way and makes the book you loved come up in more also bought searches and has the chance to be featured in consumer newsletters.

Just a quick "I loved this book" is praise enough and encourages your favorite writers to churn out that next favorite read. So don't be shy, if you enjoyed reading, a review would mean the world for a relatively new book! Follow this link to leave a review!